DEDIC⌐

Dedicated to my soul mate **Gem**

To my friends **Becci**, **Kathryn**, **Woody**, **Mel, Esther**, and **Gemma**. Thank you for the inspiration, read on, you'll see.

Alan. The bond between friends can never be broken. Not even death can part the bond of true friends.

Adam. With love. x x x

ONE

Never Before

I t has never happened before.
It may never happen again.
It is about to happen right now.

TWO
Energies Collide

The distinctive and unbearable noise of my iPhone alarm blurted out and, for a split second, my heart sank as I thought I've got fifteen minutes to get up for work. Usually, I would use the snooze button and roll over, leaving me with just twelve minutes to get up washed and dressed, and be out of the house for 05:15 am. Still, this time I got my phone out of my pocket and saw the 05:00 time stamp on the alarm and, with a smile to myself, I used my thumb to flick the notice to the left, selecting 'dismiss'.

I looked over to my mate Barkley, and my smile turned into a cheeky grin as I reached into the icebox right beside me. The beer cans were floating in a pool of lukewarm water along with a few dead insects and crumbs of food, remnants from our last camping trip.

"No work for me today," I said, as my smile turned into a cheeky grin for my mate. "The last can and then I'm going to have a couple of hours kip."

I threw Barkley the can. It was like slow motion watching the can spin 360 degrees over and over heading towards him, hurtling through the air. It was joined by an incalculable amount of water droplets from the icebox all heading in his direction like a meteor shower. His instant reaction was faultless as his right arm shot out and caught the can mid-spin, closely followed by splashes of tepid water hitting him across the face and into the eyes.

"Az!" Barkley moaned in a teenage childlike groan elongating my name to 'Aaaaaaz', wiping the water from his face.

Az, that's me. Aaron Abbey. 43 years young. Happy and content with life. My mate Barkley Brown, or BB, and I have known each other since primary school. Year four to be exact. My parents moved houses to a small village called Redgrand, North of England, in the county of Yorkshire. I moved schools and joined Yellow Class with Miss Hallam; I had just four more weeks at school before we broke up for the six-week summer holidays. For the first four years of his school life, Barkley had always been the first name read out on the register. On the first day at my new school, Miss Hallam introduced me to the class and asked me to sit on the blue table. Miss Hallam, a young teacher in her early twenties with light brown hair which fell to just above her shoulders, and a perfect straight fringe that sat just above her eyebrows, slowly and gracefully took a seat at her desk and opened the class register.

"Aaron Abbey," she said, her voice so lovingly and authoritative at the same time.

I replied with a hearty, bright, and enthusiastic, "Good morning Miss Hallam!"

In response, the entire class erupted in laughter. I wasn't aware that my new school didn't have to wish the teacher a good morning or a good afternoon. Instead, a simple 'Here Miss' met the requirements. As the laughter subsided, and Miss Hallam embraced my response yet trying to hush the class down and save my embarrassment, we heard the most whingey cry ever. Sat across from me was this boy with dark brown hair and the most significant set of dark brown eyes to match. His hair was long and rested just on the top of his shoulders, cut to just above the top of his prominent ears, which poked out of his dark wispy head of hair. His dark brown eyes were laden with tears and mucus running down his nose. The first tear landed on his He-Man jumper as Miss Hallam from her desk shrieked out, "Barkley Brown whatever is the matter?"

BB could not speak, but carried on wailing with the only recognisable word being 'first'. His sobs subsided, wiping the snot from his nose and smearing it across the bottom of the right sleeve on his He-Man jumper.

After a second, BB stated, "I'm the first name on the register; not him. I've always been first."

I leaned forward across the table and made clear, direct eye to eye contact with him. His pupils fixed on mine as I said, "Don't worry, you will always come first to me."

I don't know why I said it, or if I even meant it, but from that very moment we sealed our friendship. His face changed shape as his facial muscles started to relax from a fixed frown, stiff and angry-looking. The corners of his lips turned up until there was a big smile on his face.

We're now in our early forties, and we have made some great memories between us. Some good, some bad, but one thing that never changed was our getaway weekends. We had recently found a perfect spot for the tent, and had frequented the same place for the last six months or so. It was right on top of an old quarry; it was perfection. We could see for miles from up there, and with no light pollution. The ideal spot for camping.

The area was a conservation project back in the '60s, converting the former quarry site into grassland, woodland, and heathland providing a much-needed habitat, and the perfect place for Barkley and me to pitch our tent.

We were on our regular 'getaway weekend'. We would throw our basic no-frills tent into the boot of Barkley's car. The tent was mainly used if it rained. We usually just fell asleep in our camping chairs, our ice-cool box filled with cans of beer, disposable BBQ, and some food. Nothing too fancy. It was mainly just junk food to nibble on. On our getaway breaks, we would sit in our camp chairs, get very drunk and talk crap all night until one of us fell asleep in the chair. Our disposable BBQ would double as our campfire when we had eaten, and we'd take it in turns to go out and fetch dry wood supplies to keep it going. I say we take it in turns, but in reality, I would send Barkley out on the hunt if it was my turn; he rarely said no.

The sun was just about to break. On the far end of the horizon, there was a lighter shade of darkness in the sky. I was so tired. I'd just worked a double shift at the hospital the day before and I had not slept for nearly forty eight hours.

Barkley got up from his chair and said, "I'll just get some more wood. Let's see if I can keep this going a while longer."

By the time Barkley got back, I had finished my last can of beer.

I looked to him and said, "Right, I'm gonna have a couple of hours sleep". As I said, we usually fall asleep on the chairs, but I just wanted to lay down and stretch out a bit and put my head on a pillow. My sleeping bag had a built-in pillow; it was about five years old but was pretty much brand new, barely even used. It was purple, and when it hit the light, it had a very high golden glossy shine. It was a cheap fabric that caused me to get electric shocks whenever I turned over during the night. The static spark would illuminate the tent with a quick flicker; enough to hurt my eyes when the sharpness and brightness hit my dilated pupils. I crawled into my sleeping bag. Listening carefully, I could hear Barkley raking the new wood on the fire, and the zip on the tent door that was rolled up to one side hitting against the metallic tent pole with the breeze.

I turned over - got a static shock, and I closed my eyes.

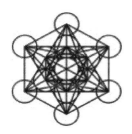

I HAD NO THOUGHTS. I had nothing. I could see nothing. I could hear nothing. I was asleep; unconscious. I was out like a light.

In the next moment, I felt like I was being electrocuted but without any pain. All of my senses became activated at one hundred percent capacity. To be honest, it felt more than one hundred percent and if there was a bigger scale to measure it on, I would. Maybe a million percent would have been more accurate. There is no other way of describing the amount of energy that came through me.

It was like a bolt of energy that entered at the back of my head, right at the top of my spine. It went straight into my pituitary gland, and straight through my hypothalamus. I did not even realise I knew what my pituitary gland or hypothalamus was, but at that moment, right then, I understood every part of my human body. I felt like I was standing in front of the most powerful amplifier at a concert as it was being turned on for the first time, booting up. It felt like the electrical energy the amplifiers convert into sound boomed into my chest.

My eyes, skin, bones, every part of my body, experienced this magnitude of vibrations travelling throughout me, my mind, and soul. Light and darkness expanded around me. Both light and dark at the same time. I could not understand how I was able to experience both light and dark, and all the colours in between, all at the same time. Up was down and down was up. My skin felt like it was on fire. Yet, I felt no pain. Every cell was alive, and I knew and could feel and experience each one in my body right down to my DNA. Past my DNA even, into my nucleotides and to every atom that made my human body. For the first time in my entire life, I was aware. I was self-aware; aware of myself in a way I didn't know was possible.

I knew I was on the floor with only the plastic base of a cheap tent and my sleeping bag between the earth and me.

I could still hear BB muttering to himself as he continued to rake the fire, keeping the embers alight. The zip on the tent door continued to clang against the aluminium pole. I was aware of my physical surroundings, aware that my eyes were closed. I could feel the sleeping bag against my skin, my chest wall would rise and fall, and I could hear my exhalation, yet I was entirely somewhere else.

It felt like I was on this marvellous drug-induced trip. However, I'd never taken drugs of any kind in the past. Not even had a cigarette. I have always been too paranoid and naïve to try anything illegal or try anything that could damage my health. Other than alcohol, of course.

The light and dark and all the colours in between started to change from my vision's centre. I could see what looked like lots of neurons right in front of my eyes. They looked like branches from a tree; pathways in a brain, like synapses moving across each component. I feel like I am one, it's all one. Everything is one. The light. The dark. The gold.

I can see an image. An outline of a pyramid pulsating. It slowly morphs into a skyscraper. At that moment, I realise that time has no connection to the past or the future. The building transforms into an image of the Earth. I am looking down onto the planet as if I am in outer space and I feel connected to the Earth like never before. Connecting. We're all one.

When I look more closely at the planet, I can see beams of light, billions of individual rays of light. It looks as if someone had pricked the Earth a billion times with a pin and in doing so created little holes letting the light escape from inside, into the darkness of space. It reminds me of a stereographic lampshade. I knew what the light beams were. They were people; I could see each single human and humanoid beings' light source. I could see their souls.

Suddenly, something pulled me in a direction. I want to describe it as being pulled forwards, but I was forwards and I was backwards. I was everything. It was like being pulled outwards; I was expanding. The earth faded into billions of colours. The colours around me formed a tunnel. It wasn't the kind that people describe in a near-death experience. It was more like a chamber. Swirls of light of all different colours surrounded me, spiralling. The light energy surrounding me was intense. I can't describe it as a feeling. 'Feeling' felt too human. In this state, there were no words to describe how I was feeling. It was pure love, light, magic, divine, words I would never use in my human life.

I knew I wasn't having a near-death experience because I was still aware of my physical body on the ground. I could have remained in this chamber of love and light for eternity.

As I floated in what seemed to be a healing chamber of some sort, one of the colours that swirled around me formed into the shape of a human hand. It was a deep orange and gold, with glimpses of red, like the sun changing colour as it greeted me. The love emanating from this hand was indescribable. No love on earth could ever meet this intensity. I wanted to hold my hand out to greet this hand, but I realised I did not have any hands at all. For the first time, I realised I was a ball of energy. I too was energy swirling around observing, loving, knowing, being. I imagined a hand of my own reaching out, and as I did, the deep orange, red and gold hand pulled me. This time, I could feel I was being pulled towards this energy force, the feeling of euphoria overwhelmed me.

I felt this presence, this energy force, observing me. Loving me. The surroundings of the healing chamber dissipated and transformed before my eyes into my childhood home. I recognised the small living room straight away. The now-dated nicotine-stained wallpaper, both my parents were big smokers. I saw my mum's ornaments and pictures hanging on the wall. The now unfashionable furniture, our grey carpet, and red rug in front of the council fitted gas fire. I was home.

I instantly knew the light being had created a place where I was at my happiest. It was a place in my life where I felt safe and secure with no worries in the world. As I took in my new surroundings, I felt the same euphoria as I had earlier. It felt like I was back on Earth, but I knew that I wasn't. This was a construct. It was a construct I felt the being had created for me. If I looked closely at my childhood living room, I could see it was like looking through the bottom of thousands and thousands of empty glass Coca-Cola bottles, with the light and colours shining through to create the illusion of my living room. It was like looking at a TV screen with a magnifying glass, and you could see all the different coloured pixels which made up the image.

I looked at my hand and realised I was still holding this hand made from light. The hand then slowly took shape as it formed an arm. A chest and torso. Legs and feet. And, lastly, a head and face.

"Hello again," the being said.

SCHUMANN RESONANCE

The Schumann Resonance is a balance of energies between the earth's core and the stratosphere where electromagnetic thunderbolts hit the earth's ground all around our planet. The power created forms a resonance of energy that bounces up and down, from the earth to the stratosphere and back again. It is like seeing an electrocardiograph (ECG) machine in hospitals. The Schumann Resonance is the pulse of the planet.

The Schumann Resonance, named after Winifred Schumann who predicted it mathematically in 1952, was something that I had never heard of, didn't need to know of, and something I would never dream I would begin to understand.

Until Now.

THREE
Metatron

I was overwhelmed by the feeling of oneness, love, and intelligence beyond my earthly comprehension. At the same time, I could hear BB on the camp chair outside the tent snoring. I was strangely complacent about being in two places at the same time.

"You are still connected to your earthly physical body. You won't remember everything. We have met many many times before... It's ok though do not try to think, just be". I knew the being, which had taken human form, as Metatron. He, I say he, but he was equally masculine and feminine; just Metatron. Metatron's sex appeared to the receiver how the receiver wanted to view him. I addressed Metatron as male, but even then, I knew this concept was a humanistic approach, and one that I did not need to have. Metatron was a being of light. He did not need to introduce himself; I knew who he was.

He was right, I had met him before, but I could not remember any previous times. It was just a sense of knowing. Like the feeling of déjà vu but unlike déjà vu, which only lasts for seconds, this was a constant continuous feeling of knowing.

Metatron was beautiful. Like a Hollywood actor or actress, but with the beauty and good looks a billion times over. His masculinity and femininity shone through in his words, his actions, and his persona. He was everything that was and everything that could be. I was in awe. At this point, I realised I was still holding his hand. I let go, took a step back, and admired him thoroughly.

Metatron was wearing a purple robe which came down to just above his ankles. The neckline was a band of radiant gold that glimmered and seemed to have a life of its own; shimmering and moving. It looked like golden waves were crashing outwards from his neckline. I noticed just a glimpse of chest hair, but weirdly, this still did not confirm that he was male.

His low-cut shoes exposed his ankles, and I noticed his shoes were just like the band around the neckline of the robe. Gold in colour, glimmering and shifting and changing. It was like clouds with different intensities of golds swirling in and round his shoes. Within the purple-looking material of the robe, was a golden interwoven silk thread. It started from the neckline, spreading across his chest heading downwards so that all the gold threads met at the bottom of his robe to one point, like an upside-down pyramid. The gold thread had energy running up and down it, like an electrical current covering his robe. The gold energy was pulsating and moving around its surface. It was hypnotic to watch. The gold pulse spat out at times in slow motion, like watching a solar flare from our sun. On his right shoulder hung a paludamentum, a cloak that fastened over the right shoulder, pinned together by a gold badge that had the symbol of Metatron's Cube.

How did I know what Metatron's Cube was? I don't know I just did.

Metatron had the brightest blue eyes with a hint of the most magical purple around the edges. They made you feel like you wanted to fall into them and swim for miles, such beauty and honesty emanated from them. His light brown, golden blonde hair was swept back off his forehead and hung down towards the back of his head, resting on his shoulders. His hair was so straight and perfect; not one hair out of place. His skin was a dark golden-brown with glimpses of gold scattered here and there as if he had just walked into a glitter bomb. The gold embers in his skin were very subtle, but I could see them. Again, I was in awe.

"Do you recognise this place?" He asked.

I nodded, "I lived here as a child." I pointed to my A-Team action figures, they sat in a group on the settee. It was as if I had left them there having a team meeting. They were waiting for me to finish my lunch in the dining room, for me to pick up and carry on with our adventures. "Those were the old toys I used to play with."

"You created this construct," he said. "You needed to feel safe and secure as we have this, our first meeting while you are still with blood."

"With blood?" I asked, unsure why he was mentioning blood when I did not have any physical body.

He continued, "You have not left your earthly human physical body. You are still with blood. This is the first time you have met me with blood. Not only that, but this is also the first time the earth's pulse, the life source of the earth, has passed through a living creature; a human. You, Aaron Abbey. It has passed through you."

No sooner had Metatron finished the sentence; it was as if he had downloaded into my consciousness the knowledge of the Schumann Resonance. I understood everything that had happened to me on earth while I was asleep on the ground. Energy enters the earth in the form of lightning all over the world in different time zones. This energy then exits the earth, back out to the stratosphere in a continuous circle of life energy for the cosmos. The exit points on planet earth are random and never in the same place again. I just happened to be laid in the right place at the right time of this so-called exit heartbeat, or the exit pulsation, of the earth which went straight through my pituitary gland.

Metatron went on, "The pituitary gland is associated with higher awareness and higher consciousness; it is the interconnectedness component of your earthly time's understanding of Maslow's Hierarchy. Just as the pituitary interconnects the endocrine glands to each other, so does it relate to our awareness and consciousness. Our connectedness to one another."

All this information was a knowing, like I had downloaded Wikipedia. I knew and understood everything that had happened. Still, just before I hit that pillow and went to sleep, I did not even know what Maslow's Hierarchy was, nevermind the Schumann Resonance.

"Your soul's purpose is about to begin," Metatron said. "Each decision you make will change the course or the path of many souls to come; your own included. Do not be afraid, do not let your ego take control because whichever path you make, wherever your purpose takes you; you should follow. There is no right or wrong direction. There is no right or wrong decision, ever."

"My purpose? What do you mean?" I knew what Metatron meant. I could feel the conversation in the form of a song all around me. The energy was uplifting. I did not feel frightened, or unsure, or have any doubts about any of this new information. I knew my destiny before he even opened his mouth and spoke. My life was about to change. But the human part of me wanted him to tell me my purpose; to say it out loud so that I could hear it in a form that I recognised.

"Everything humans and humanoids do, from picking a flower, to stamping on an ant, to turning left instead of right, replying to a text message instantly or later. Everything you think, pray, sing, speak, do, everything is a form of energy that integrates within this universe's geometry. The energy created from Earth forms part of the interconnected cosmos, which is feeding other solar systems. The earth processes these energies; these vibrations created by the cosmic constructs of energies and frequencies. It then digests them. Aaron, the earth is a living planet, and once digested, it then sends the energy to parts of the earth that needs it the most. The earth is forever evolving, healing, and growing. It has its own life force. The pulse that the earth expels outwards into the cosmos, the same vibrational pulse that went straight through your pituitary gland, is the force that feeds the rest of the neighbouring solar systems. It's a continuous life force.

"Your human life is about to change. Your world is about to change forever. How you embrace these changes is entirely up to you, but a change is upon you. Remember, there is no right or wrong way. I will be here as your guide. Feel your higher self, be your higher self, see your higher self. It will be difficult to connect at first, but earth time is on your side".

When Metatron said, 'see your higher self', I turned to look in the mirror which hung on the side of the chimney breast in this illusion of a living room from my childhood. In front of it was a tall square table made from mahogany. It was a small square hallway table that would generally have a telephone on. Instead, I could see my mum's hairbrush and hair spray which she would use to do her hair every morning before taking me to school. I know I didn't need to look in the mirror because as soon as Metatron uttered these words, I was fully aware of how my higher self looked. I had the same robe on as Metatron, dark purple with gold energy pulsating up and down to a point in the gold woven fabric. I had the same glowing gold shoes and a similar gold cloak on my right shoulder. What was interesting, and intriguing, was how my body looked.

I have never been one for vanity. But my hair was dark brown and had the newly noticeable odd grey hair dotted around since I'd hit my forties. It was tidy but messy, with no particular style. It was longer on top and shorter at the sides and back. I guess you could say my hair always looked windswept. I had a trimmed beard, not that I shaped it or anything. I just used my electric shaver every few days, to keep it short. The beard matched my hair perfectly; dark brown with flecks of grey. My best feature was my eyes; deep blue. Everyone would always comment on my eyes. *Honest eyes, blue eyes. Are your eyes really that colour?*

My nose was just the right size in proportion to my face, but it had what I called the 'bobble end'. No perfect magazine model ski slope nose for me. Instead, my nose resembled one of the character pieces from the old board game Cluedo. It didn't bother me as such. I would say I just looked ok. I never got bullied for my looks or anything, but my late Grandad had a big bobble end nose. I was afraid of my bobble nose getting bigger as I got older. It never did, thankfully. I had two piercings in my left ear, which I'd had done at the age of sixteen rebelling against my mother. I was in shape, but didn't work out or anything, no six-pack - never had one, no muscles to show off in my arms. I wasn't too thin or too fat. Never watched my weight. I just ate and drank what I wanted when I wanted, I guess my job at the hospital helped me to keep the weight off. I was just me, and I was happy being me.

But when I looked in the mirror and saw my reflection as the higher self me. WOW.

My hair was long and slicked back off my face. It landed at either side of my shoulders, flicking outwards. I had the same colour hair as Metatron, light golden brown with strands of gold. But, in contrast, Metatron's hair was entirely slicked back and straight. Mine had some waves in it and flicked out at the sides and the back. I had a gold headband, holding my hair back off my face. It had seven golden squares turned around so that they looked more like a diamond shape than a square. It almost looked like a king's crown. Inside each golden square was a jewel of a different colour.

The colours on the headband flowed, from left to right, violet, indigo, blue, green, yellow, orange and red. Each gemstone felt like it had a life force inside it swirling and changing colour as if you had just mixed a white loaded paintbrush into different bright colours. Or, the effect when you add milk to a coffee and the colour swirls around. Only then, I noticed my face. I had what I would call a perfect nose. The straight nose that I'd always dreamed of. My eyes were still the same shape, the same colour, but a hint of purple around the edges was evident just like Metatron's. My face had not changed apart from my hair, my ski-slope nose, the purple hue in my eyes, and I was now clean-shaven. Oh, and both my ears were hole-free. Not one trace of a piercing being present.

I looked at my arms and my chest, and I looked like I'd bulked up and been at the gym or on steroids, either way, I had definition in me. Even though I could see all this in the mirror, I did not need to visualise it. I knew how I looked. I felt it from the first instance I met Metatron.

Metatron floated up to me and spoke behind me whilst I looked into the mirror.

"Your powers will be earthbound only and have been given to you by the wisdom of the universe. Use them well. Use them wisely. Find your purpose."

Slowly, my old living room began dissolving; it was fading away. I turned around from the mirror. Metatron had gone. I could still feel the love, the energy, the beauty of life. Soon, I was in complete darkness. It was as if I had just watched a movie and the movie screen had faded to black before the credits rolled. As I lay there in the darkness, I was fully aware of BB snoring in the camp chair outside the tent.

I peeled open my eyes and took the deepest of breaths in, as if I had just swum a length of the swimming pool without coming up for air.

I gathered my surroundings, adjusted my eyes to the sunlight shining into the tent.

"What the actual...."

METATRON'S CUBE

Metatron's cube has thirteen spheres held together by lines from the mid-point of each sphere. It is said it holds the vibrational frequencies of creation starting with colour, then sounds, and then physical matter. The thirteen spheres of Metatron's cube are present throughout every aspect of our lives; be it Body, Mind, or Spirit.

FOUR
Am I Awake?

I sat up and gazed out of the tent, scraped my hair back out of my eyes and ruffled it back with my fingers to keep it in that position. Some of it fell back onto my forehead; I didn't care. Looking out, I could see the disposable BBQ with remnants of burned-out charcoal logs and branches that were now grey and white. The faintest of smoke came from its ashes. BB was fast asleep in the camp chair. I could tell his mouth was open wide by the sound of his snoring. His arms hung down either side of the camp chair. Empty cans were crushed and then strewn across our camping area.

We always cleaned up afterwards, when packing up to go home, but during our drinking fest, it felt manly to crush our cans and throw them when we had finished before cracking the next one open. As I was about to get up and head towards my empty camping chair, I saw something move from the corner of my eye. I sat still and waited, then I saw a brown rabbit run off into the undergrowth and out of sight.

I yawned, unzipped my sleeping bag, and poked my head out of the tent. I took a deep breath stood up and stretched, reaching upwards to the sky as far as I could until I could hear my back crack. I needed to pee. So, looking around just in case some walker was nearby, I walked around to the back of the tent. Picking up a few empty cans, and throwing them in the empty cooler, I carried on walking towards the tall tree that shadowed the tent.

As I stood there watering the shrubs and grass weeds growing from the base of the tree, I had a sudden flashback to my dream. I could hear Metatron in a loud overpowering voice as if he was stood right next to me, "Feel your higher self. Be your higher self. See your higher self."

I finished mid pee and zipped up quickly; I honestly felt as if somebody was stood behind me.

"What the..." I said as I turned around half expecting BB to be standing behind me, joking around at my expense. No-one was there.

I looked around the area to see if I could see anyone else. Thoughts were running around my head, I thought to myself, 'I bet I was talking in my sleep and now someone is making a joke of me'. But there was no one in sight. Nothing. Just silence, apart from a bird chirp coming from the tree above. I got out my iPhone just to check that my YouTube app wasn't playing or something. It wasn't. I unlocked it using my facial recognition and checked the time, it was only 8:58 am. I'd had just enough sleep to get by for the rest of the day. It would be an early night for me though. I had a double shift again tomorrow at work.

Scratching the back of my neck and squinting, I thought to myself, "How on earth did I just hear that sentence from my dream? Am I still dreaming? Am I still drunk?"

I repeated the phrase back to myself, "Feel your higher self. Be your higher self. See your higher self."

I chuckled and walked back to my camp chair, throwing myself into it. I fell back into it without giving myself any support. I sat there and wondered about my dream, flashbacks of Metatron, my pixelated living room. I reflected on how weird the experience was. I reached for a bottle of water from the cup holder in the chair. I'd already opened the bottle last night and taken a quick drink from it to take two paracetamols. I always took paracetamol before drinking, or during drinking, alcohol. It's preventative; for the hangover.

My friends would call me the paracetamol king as I always had them to hand and would take them even if I had the slightest bit of pain. I unscrewed the plastic top from the water bottle and took a swig of the water. Again, I started thinking about the dream I had just had. It had created thoughts that would linger with me all day.

I closed my eyes and remembered the part of the dream when I was in what felt like space, with all the colours swirling around me. At that precise moment, whilst I was thinking about being in the air, I felt like all my cells had come alive. I felt a glowing both surrounding and becoming me. It was like I was on fire again but with no pain.

I opened my eyes, and I did have this luminous glow surrounding my body. My hands, my legs, my arms. I was encircled within this glow that shone brightly. The light was a brilliant gold, with yellows and golds shifting outwards like the sea hitting the shore. I felt my energy, my frequency, had synced with the universe. It was happening at the same time I was thinking of being in space in my dream. Without warning, without a feeling, or even a knowing, I was floating up out of my chair.

I tried to grip onto the only thing I could, and that was the plastic water bottle in my hand. Water spilt out all over me. Was I still dreaming?

I did, however, feel safe. It was a weird feeling to have when I was floating above my friend surrounded by an orange glow. I could not control what was happening, but I didn't feel frightened or scared.

I was now above the treetops. I could see the bird that had watched me pee.

I still felt like I was in the dream. I had a little laugh to myself, I did a flip in the air, and I felt like a child let loose for the first time on a trampoline. I took in the view, I could see for miles. I looked in all directions. In the distance, I could see the building where I worked. Redgrand District Hospital. It was about eight, maybe even ten miles away, but it was the tallest building in our town and stuck out like a sore thumb. It was always the first building you would see, set back in the distance, if you were driving back home on the motorway.

I looked at the building. I tried to focus on it. Suddenly, my vision started to zoom in, like a TV show where the camera would slowly zoom in on an item. Only this was in double speed, and my vision zoomed in within seconds. I could see the building as if I was stood right outside it. I looked up to one of the wards where my friend worked. Leigh Clark was one of my closest friends. I'd go as far as to say she was my soul mate. We became close after studying French together in high school, we both failed the exam after two years of supposed study. We didn't care for it, but we cared for each other.

I zoomed in on one of the windows, which I knew was the floor where her ward was. I could see her as clear as day. She was taking a blood pressure reading on a patient. I could not hear the conversation, but I had this feeling that if I'd have wanted to be there, I could be in an instant. Leigh was a beautiful person inside and out, hence I think why she studied hard and became a nurse. She was always caring for others, putting them ahead of herself.

Leigh had a round figure that suited her personality. She was lively and bubbly. She had the most exceptional laugh, that had the power to make you fall into laughter too. Even if you were not in on the joke, you would laugh out loud at her raucous laughter.

Leigh looked out of the window, not one of those looks where you take in the view. One of those looks where you look to see if somebody is watching you. Right then, without warning, I could see her look directly into my eyes. I did freak out a little and screamed out loud. Suddenly, the video camera that was my eyes, zoomed back so fast it nearly made me sick. The golden glow that emanated from my body had gone, and I was falling.

I landed in the camping chair, which on impact spread out with all four legs akimbo. I did not hurt myself. I was astonished to say the least. No words came out of my mouth. Barkley woke and saw me flat out on the floor on top of the crumpled camp chair and started laughing so hard he nearly wet himself. I could see the tears in his eyes running down his face. I began to laugh with him, realising that he had just witnessed the chair collapsing and not the height from which I had just fallen.

Just then a bottle of water came landing down on top of me, bounced off my stomach, and upon impact, forced the remaining water out of the bottle up into the air landing all over my face. Barkley was laughing more than ever. I have never seen him laugh so much. I was in shock, but I was still laughing with him. Just then my iPhone alerted me to a text; I slid out my phone, I clicked into it. It was a message from Leigh. It read, "Just thinking about you - love you, pal."

We packed up, collected the rubbish, and poured water on the BBQ. We threw it all into a black plastic bin bag along with the wrecked camping chair and put it into the back of BB's Mini Cooper Sport. It wasn't his car. It was Kim's; his girlfriend. But he used it more than she did. It was practically his, just not by name.

We got in the car and set off for home. I didn't speak all the way home. BB would usually call off at a garage and top the car up with petrol, and I'd offer half payment, but he didn't this time, he just drove. Radio 2 blurted out it was nearly 9:30 am and Zoe Ball was just signing off her breakfast show. She was talking to Ken Bruce, the presenter of the next show. She asked him if he slept well last night, it must have been a running topic of conversations she had had during her show.

"Strangely," he said over the car radio, "I slept very well thank you."

With that, BB turned the radio off and said, "I slept well last night as well, even though I only probably had about two hours of sleep. I feel as if I have slept for weeks. I feel so revitalised, full of energy, I feel as if I could run a marathon."

Silence fell upon us again. I didn't engage with his conversation. I couldn't stop thinking of how I saw Leigh from eight miles away and how it felt like she saw me. I couldn't comprehend that I was floating above the trees. My mind was racing away with itself. I thought to myself, "I'll see Leigh tomorrow at work. I'll ask her if she saw me, or I'll ask her why she sent me the text."

"You're quiet," BB said.

"I slept well too," was my reply.

We pulled up outside my house, and I said I'd take the trash out from the boot of his car as it was my bin collection day tomorrow; living on my own my bin is hardly ever half full. I gave BB a nod and a slight wave as his driver's side window wound down and his right arm rested on the ledge, "Cheers BB. I'll message you later mate," I said as he drove off.

I live on a new-build estate, well I say new build, my house is five years old now, and I am the first person to live in it. It's just big enough for me. You could call it a two up two down. It is semi-detached with no front garden, only a drive off the road leading up to my house from the main street. My back garden, however, is a different matter. That is my retreat, my quiet zone where I often go and sit by my pond and listen to the water fountain, watching the fish swim around. It's where I go to reflect and zone out on world matters. Inside my house, I would say my decor was quite trendy, minimalistic, everything has its place.

One of my friends Charlotte Kallel, or 'Lottie' as she likes to be called, has been a part of my life for many years. We used to work together during our teenage years in a care home as healthcare workers. We have both moved on since then, our lives took different paths. Lottie has done a lot with her life. She got married and had three children, two of them are twins, they are now thirteen years old. Even as our lives changed, we stayed friends. She would often invite me round for a meal with her family. I'd usually return the favour, and I can hear her now calling me a 'Clean Freak' or she'd say 'I'm sure you've got OCD'. I wouldn't go that far but living on your own for so long, no kids to make a mess, I guess she just sees my house as a bit tidier than hers.

Next door attached to my house lives a lovely old gentleman, called Mr Williams. John, as he insists I call him, even though I still call him

Mr Williams. He is a retired music teacher, a reticent man, down to earth, and you can sometimes hear him tinkling away on his ivories now and again. I think his wife must have died sometime before moving into our new build houses. I could not ask for a better neighbour. He would often drop me a note and ask me to get him some groceries. I didn't mind at all. I've always liked to do my best for people.

I took the rubbish through the house as it was easier than walking around to unlock the back gate. I opened the back-patio double doors, walked through the garden and placed the black sack and crumpled camp chair in the big grey wheeled bin. I fed my goldfish and sprinkled the feed across the pond. Twelve hungry mouths came flooding to the top, each one splashing as they opened their mouths above the water's surface. I watched for a minute or two as they swam up, took the food, and swam back down, repeating until there was no food left floating on the water. For those two minutes watching the fish, my mind was at rest. For the first time, my mind was not thinking of how I floated above BB. I didn't know if I had finally lost it, but it didn't feel like I'd been hallucinating.

My rapid thoughts soon snapped back, and with my mind racing again, I returned to the kitchen. I poured some filtered water into my kettle and flicked the switch to make myself a coffee. I needed a coffee. I needed a strong coffee.

I used two scoops of instant Nescafé Gold instead of the usual one spoon. I added the boiling water to my Superman mug and then poured in some milk from the fridge, choosing to sit in my favourite armchair, in the kitchen. I didn't even put the milk back in the refrigerator. My mind was on other things.

My armchair was another one of my safe zones. It was a high back retro-looking chair, in Queen Anne's style with the high back curving inwards at the top. When I first bought it, Lottie called it my 'nursing home chair'. You could always count on Lottie to wind me up. Sat in my so called 'nursing home chair', positioned facing the double patio doors that looked onto the garden, I could see and hear my fountain in the pond. I had a little side table where I would put my book or drink just to the right of me. This was my thinking chair. I loved it. Come rain or shine, this chair was my indoor relaxing place.

I sat down with my strong coffee and tried to make sense of what had happened earlier this morning. Was I going mad? Did I need to see my doctor? Did it happen? Was it imagined?

I remembered the dream, and I remembered 'Metatron', and the feeling of love that overcame me again. I remember seeing my living room as it was when I was a child. The things Metatron had said to me. I thought to myself, "I could not make these things up even if I tried." I have a limited imagination. I don't have any form of artistic intelligence of any state. Where, in my imagination, did I pull out this dream? So many questions remain unanswered.

I took a drink from my coffee cup and saw the Superman logo. I laughed at myself. "Don't be stupid!" I said out loud. I was not a super-hero fan; it was not my genre of entertainment. I liked an excellent psychological thriller, if I ever did watch a movie, or a good James Bond. But not comic books turned movies, especially not Superman. The Superman mug was a housewarming gift from Leigh, she bought it for me as this was my first house purchase. She thought I was all grown up and now a responsible adult even though I was thirty seven when I bought the house. The mug came with a pair of Superman socks, which went straight to the charity shop, and a beautiful card calling me Superman for being all grown up buying my first house. Bless my mate, Leigh.

Looking at the mug, and then to my hand holding it, I put the cup down and held both of my hands up in front of me. I turned them back and forth and then I had this daft thought, "Okay, let's see." I imagined gold coming out of me and surrounding me like it was when I was floating above Barkley this morning. Nothing.

I closed my eyes, thought about the gold light coming out of me, strained my face as if pushing out something that wasn't even there, opened one eye to take a peek at my hands, nothing.

I shook my head in disbelief at myself, "Aaron, what are you doing?"

I put my hands down and looked into my garden. I admired my flowers, not that I am green-fingered or anything, but this summer my garden had taken on a life of its own. Right at the bottom, leaning up to the fence in a rockery patch that I had created last summer, I had some yellow Little Dorrits which had just come into flower. Little Dorrit is a dwarf variety of sunflower, growing to a height of only 60cm. I could see a bumblebee flying around, with a distance of about twenty meters between me and the flowers.

I looked closely at the bee which had landed on one of the flower heads. I can't believe I was going to try, but I did, I tried to zoom in. I tried to get a closer look, focused my eyes on the bumblebee, I imagined a camera lens turning so my zoom vision would zoom in. I strained my eyes so hard I could feel my veins pumping out at my temples. I tried this a couple of times. Nothing. Zilch.

I finally said to myself, "Aaron, you have lost it; you have finally gone and lost it."

I drank my coffee, looked at my iPhone, it had a red battery symbol. I plugged it in and left it on the kitchen worktop, "Time for a shower," I thought to myself.

The day went by pretty quickly, I did a few odd jobs around the house, watered my indoor plants, nothing too strenuous, it was after all my last day off for a few days. I ironed a couple of my uniform polo shirts for work. It was a royal blue polo neck t-shirt. I made sure I got the iron right into the nooks of the embroidered logo. It read 'Redgrand District Hospital' in yellow embroidery at the top in a semi-circle, above an outline of the hospital building. At the bottom, it read 'Portering Services' in red lettered embroidery.

I was a porter at the hospital and had been since I was eighteen. After twenty five years, everyone knew me, even the regular patients on the various wards. I don't want to sound pretentious because that's not me, but I was popular. I didn't need to feel popular, or require it, I guess because I had worked there for so long, since being a teenager, everyone knew me or knew of me. Twenty five years was a bloody long time. I was a part of the furniture. Everyone knows Aaron Abbey; always happy to oblige.

Redgrand Hospital was all I had ever known. The portering department used to be part of the NHS. However, the estate's department, which the portering services came under, was privatised after three years of campaigning to prevent it. Since the privatisation, I took voluntary redundancy. Since then, I've worked as an agency worker, still doing the same job, same shifts, but 'agency work' which means I do not have a contract with the National Health Service. I can pick and choose the shifts I work. I get roughly the same income; actually, I do get slightly more, as I can choose to work the weekend, or after 8 pm into the night shift, as these shifts pay more. The more hours I work, the more I accrue paid annual leave, so basically, I got a tidy lump sum of cash from my redundancy, which I put straight into savings. Now, I choose when I want to work, deciding my hours as and when. A-Lex services is a global agency, and I could, if I wanted to, work anywhere in the world, as long as they had contracts with the hospitals. However, I have never worked anywhere else, but who knows, maybe one day I might head down south and work a week in Brighton and then take a holiday. I'm full of these little ideas, but never actually do anything about them. Twenty five years I've been in the same job, I've had more managers than I have years worked there, but I like it. I still wear my old NHS royal blue porters' uniform; no one says anything. The agency uniform is bright red with the agency's name embroidered on the left side chest. 'A-LEX SERVICES', in bright yellow embroidery offset against the bright red polo neck t-shirt. I'd gotten my agency uniform when I started work with them three years ago, but my NHS ones still had plenty of life left in them.

I prepared my packed lunch, ready for work tomorrow, brown bread, cheese, and ham, no butter just a dry sandwich. I had never liked butter as far as I can remember. I placed it in a plastic bag and put it in the fridge. I checked on my iPhone, I'd had three missed calls and three unread text messages. My battery was on one hundred percent. I took my phone upstairs and jumped into bed. I set my alarm for 05:00 am. I checked my missed calls. They were all from Leigh, no voice message left. I read my three messages; again, all three were from Leigh.

13:03: "Are you ok?"

15:56: "Just on my break, ring me!"

20:45: "In bed, Pal, I'll see you at work tomorrow."

I thought about my dream last night with Metatron. The feelings I felt of euphoria, the empowering words he spoke to me; it felt so real, more than just an ordinary dream. I let my mind wander onto this morning's events. It was clear to me now that this morning was a dream as well. It must have been.

I took a quick look at my Facebook. It was kind of a ritual, it would be the last thing I do most nights. Scrolling up and seeing everyone's life flash past me with a swish of my thumb. It just seemed to put me in a relaxed state. I might update my Facebook status on the odd occasion but I don't usually post loads of things. I'm more of a Facebook lurker than anything, but I decided to post just before I went to sleep.

Aaron Abbey

What's on your mind?

'Yet another amazing getaway break with my mate BB. Again, we put the world to rights, moaned, and got very drunk. Here's to the next one - Night Peeps!'

I then uploaded a selfie of us both to the status and tagged BB in it, with our tent in the background, BB holding up a can of beer, with big grins on our faces. There was a purple and gold shaft of light vertically running down the picture right next to me. It must be a lens flare.

FIVE
Healing Caroline

The alarm kicked in, and before I knew it, I was ready and packed for work, and getting my mountain bike out of the shed. It only took ten minutes to get to work. If it was raining, or if we had ice or snow, I would opt for a taxi.

I arrived at work, slid my bike into one of the cycle shelters, secured my helmet while passing the chain through the holes, and locked it up.

I always entered through A&E. You could tell if you were going to have a busy shift or not by the number of ambulances parked up in front of the Accident & Emergency department. If there were a lot, and by a lot, I mean more than eight, this meant a couple of things, either there had been a major incident, which was very rare in our small town, or the hospital was full. Capacity was at maximum, so ambulance teams were waiting in the A&E car park to hand over a patient to the nursing and medical team. It was like a conveyor belt, either waiting for a patient to die on one of the wards, or self-discharge, or transfer to another hospital, or just be discharged. In doing so, this would then free up a bed on the ward, allowing an ambulance to discharge a patient to the A&E department.

Today was going to be a good day; there was only one ambulance outside as I entered the automatic sliding doors. It was just pulling out onto the main road with its crew ready to save more lives.

"Morning," I said to Jeanette on reception, as I whisked past.

"Morning love," she said, putting the phone down and then greeting the next patient in line.

As porters, we had our own changing rooms. I still had my original locker, even though I was now agency, they let me keep it. I took off my tracksuit top and pulled out my royal blue polo neck uniform, freshly ironed, and slipped it on. I opened my locker and got out my ID badge. It was neon yellow with the NHS Trust's name across the bottom. At the top, it read 'Hello, my name is' and then my name 'Aaron Abbey' across the middle. I should wear my 'A-LEX SERVICES' ID badge, but I still choose to wear my original name badge. No one says anything, not even my boss.

I saw some of the other lads just entering the changing room as I was just about to clock in.

"Morning Az."

"Morning Shep," I replied, followed by a bit of pleasant banter. The lads carried on talking about the football match that played out last night. Clocking in was a lot easier than it used to be. We used mini-iPads. We simply collected an iPad from the charging doc and logged in. I would log in to the A-Lex App; this would time stamp my shift starting. The iPad would be yours for the entire shift. The jobs would come up in time order onto all of our iPads throughout the day. There were usually ten porters on duty during the day shift, in reality, there should be fourteen, but it was uncommon that the portering department was ever fully staffed.

Our iPads would alert us to a new job. There could be up to thirty five jobs waiting at any one time during the busiest part of the day. Priority jobs were in red, and this mainly involved moving a patient from one area to another, or equipment that was needed urgently. These priority jobs had to be done, obviously, as a priority, and the blue jobs would get done as soon as possible, these were the jobs that stacked up. It was all automated, gone were the days when a supervisor would sit in the office and co-ordinate us throughout the shift using a bleep system. Anyone who needed a porter would go to their computer screen and book a job without using a coordinator, this job would then go to all our iPads. Whoever was booking a porter would code it 'urgent' or 'non-urgent', and a short description of what was required.

Leigh worked on 'Ward 29'. It was a medical assessment unit, we got a lot of jobs from Ward 29. It was either taking patients to other departments as part of their medical diagnostics, x-ray, phlebotomy, and discharge lounge. Sometimes, we'd get the call to take a patient to 'Rose Cottage'. Rose Cottage was the code name for the hospital morgue. "Hopefully no visits for Rose Cottage today," I thought to myself.

I'd just signed in and clocked on, and my first job popped up on my iPad.

Dept: Ward 29

Sender: RGN Clark

Requirement: Take blood samples to labs (air pod broken).

It was from Leigh, and she had used our code (air pod broken). Even if the pod was working, this was her way of letting me know she wanted me to pick this job regardless of the other non-priority jobs. She knew I was on duty, and she needed to speak to me.

I accepted the job. Leigh will have the kettle already on the boil in the staff room.

I took the stairs, it was only two levels up from our changing room. The entrance read 'Welcome to Ward 29' in big letters above the double doors. Before I even got the chance to open them, she was there. She wore a blue coloured nurses' uniform, with two pockets on either side at the hips, and one on her chest's right side. She had a pair of scissors, a black biro pen, a red biro pen, and a highlighter poking out from the top. Her photo ID name badge turned around so you could not see her picture, you could just see a barcode. She hated that photo. She stood there, hair tied up in a messy knot on top of her head, her eyelashes were heavily dosed in mascara, often with big clumps on the ends flicking up and down as she blinked.

"I say," she said in a kind of 'come here I've got some gossip for you' way. "Don't think I have gone mad, will you? Because if you do, then I probably have gone mad." She said, "Look, I know this is going to sound weird, and I mean weird, but bear with me, and hear me out."

"So," she continued, "yesterday, I was taking a patient's blood pressure in bed 23 and..."

She stopped mid-sentence, she could see the colour draining from my face, I leaned on the handrail on the wall, which is usually for the elderly to use. I knew what she was going to say. I didn't want to know, I didn't want her to carry on. I composed myself.

"Are you ok, pal?" she asked.

"Yeah, I'm good. I just didn't sleep well last night, and I missed breakfast this morning." This was a complete lie as I had slept like a baby and I don't usually make breakfasts anyway. Leigh knew this but didn't say anything; she carried on.

"Anyway, I'm taking this fella's blood pressure, and I just happen to look out of the window and, no word of a lie, I saw this man outside the window looking straight in at me."

"And?" I said, as if to say what's this got to do with me.

She says, "We're on Level 4, pal." She looks around to check no one else can hear our conversation. She repeats, holding four fingers up to me. "Four, you think that's weird?" She carried on, and lowered her voice even more, "The man that was floating outside the window. It was you Az, I swear to god it was you. He didn't look like you though. He had longer hair than you, and to be fair, it was a lighter brown than yours. Oh, and his nose wasn't yours, I guess he had your eyes and mouth."

"Ok," she released, "So he didn't look like you, but I just know it was you. I just had this feeling, pal, it freaked me out!" She stood there, waiting for my reaction, hands on her hips. I didn't say anything.

"Oh, and he had this luminous gold light shining out of him."

I didn't know what to say; I didn't know what to do. I cracked a smile, and this turned into a chuckle, then into a belly laugh. Leigh joined in, and her raucous laughter boomed out. "Pal," she said. "I'm serious. I know what I saw."

I gave her a look as if to say without words, "Come on! Really?"

She looked at her fob watch and took note of the time. "I've lost it, pal. The lid has finally flipped, I have finally gone and lost it. Text me when you get your lunch notification, and I'll see if I can break off at the same time. I'll meet you in the canteen later."

And with that, she hurried off down the ward heading to one of the cubicle rooms with a red light above the door. A patient had used the nurse call buzzer and required assistance.

I could not quite catch my breath. My throat and mouth had gone dry, and I did feel as if my knees had gone weak. Leigh had just confirmed what I was telling myself was a dream. She made it apparent that what happened was not a dream. How can she have shared the same vision as me? She was awake, she was at work, and was busy, and she saw what I experienced.

It happened. It was real. I headed straight back to the porter's locker room and straight to the toilet. I tried to be sick, but nothing would come up. I tried to spit but nothing. I was so dry-mouthed, it felt like I'd woken up after a night on the beer. I took a plastic cup from the drink water dispenser and drunk it, then a second, and then a third.

My iPad was bleeping as the jobs were coming in. I had to sit down. I cradled my head in my hands and ruffled my hair. I guess if anyone saw me, they would think I had just seen my favourite football team lose. Not that I followed football much, I would support my local football team, Redgrand's red and whites, but I wasn't a fan. We were bottom of the league, but whenever we played, it was the talk of the porters' staff room, so I joined in with the lad's banter and comments. I was more a tennis fan. I'd religiously record it if I was working and watch the game when I got home.

"Oh my god," I said to myself out loud, "Did this happen?"

I went back to Leigh's conversation in my head. She described me, but not me. The description she gave of the 'not me' person floating, the more I thought about it, matched what I looked like in my dream when I was with Metatron. This discussion we had had was making me anxious, and I started to take shallow breaths, nearly going into a panic attack. Part of me wished that Barkley had been awake to see and experience the same thing so that I could share what I was going through. Instead, the only witness was Leigh, who happened to have been miles away at the time. I put my head into my hands again, ruffled my hair, and took a deep breath.

I had laughed it off with Leigh, maybe she might never mention it again. I thought about what Leigh had said, and how she does not know that I experienced the same. I decided to do some more digging at lunch-time, and see exactly what she knew. I looked at my mini-iPad, which had been bleeping consistently throughout my mini break down. It read...

Dept: X-ray

Sender: RGN Kent

Requirement: Return the patient to Ward 30.

I clicked accept and set off to the x-ray department.

I kept myself busy during the first half of my shift. The Accident & Emergency department was getting busier, so there were many transfers of patients from A&E to Ward 29. I didn't see Leigh again to chat to. We were both busy with our jobs. I tried not to think about any of the events or what Leigh had said to me this morning. I just got on with my daily routine, remaining as pleasant as I could be as I transferred patients and equipment to and fro. I kept a smile on my face. No one wanted to be in the hospital, most of all the staff that worked there. But being a patient, being unwell, having to stay away from their loved ones until they recovered, or having their illness diagnosed wasn't a pleasant experience for anyone. I always tried to put a smile on their face as well, no matter what. It was just the way I was. Today was different though, I went around and did my job, but I was quiet. Very quiet.

When my iPad alert went off, it was 13:00. It made a different sound. This time, it was a long beep, different from the sound it makes when a job gets posted. It was the notification message to say it was my turn to take my lunch break. I messaged Leigh to tell her I was going on my lunch break. She didn't reply. Sometimes she could make it, others not, it all depended on how busy her shift was, how many admissions she had, how many discharges she had. If she had a critically ill patient that she could not leave. The variables changed depending on how the ward was. As she didn't reply, I didn't expect to see her when I got to the canteen, but I did. There she was.

I sat down beside her with my pre-prepared packed lunch from yesterday. I placed it out on a paper napkin and unscrewed my flask of coffee.

Leigh had been to the counter and was tucking into a full English breakfast. Even though it was gone one pm. Leigh dipped a piece of toast into the yolk of one of her two fried eggs.

"Got to keep the carbs up, pal. It's gonna be a long shift," she said as she delicately placed the yolk ladened piece of toast into her mouth.

"I thought you wouldn't be able to make it," I said as I took a bite into my dry ham and cheese sandwich.

"I've got a student nurse on with me, she's shit hot. I'm working alongside Sister Lana today so between them both, the ward is in good hands. I feel like I can take a step back, so I have! I'm treating myself to a decent breakfast for my lunch."

We both sat there for a few minutes in silence as we ate our lunch. I didn't know how to bring up the conversation we'd had this morning. I wanted to ask in more detail what the man looked like to her? What was he wearing? What was this luminous gold light? I wanted to compare notes to see if what Leigh saw out of the window was what I experienced during my dream. Did she see the other version of me? It sounded like it, but I needed more proof.

She tore into three sachets of sugar from the side of her saucer all at the same time and poured them into her tea, and she used a wooden stick stirrer to stir it in.

"About this floating or flying person that was me but wasn't me that you saw outside the window yesterday..."

I barely finished my sentence before she bit my head off and snapped right back at me. "Pal, I don't want to talk about it, ever again. I was having some kind of a senior moment. God knows what I saw, but I don't want to talk about it. I wish I never told you about it now; I feel daft as it is. Let's just leave it."

She took a big slurp from her teacup, put it down, looked at me, and said in a barely audible voice, "Whoever, or whatever, he was, he had some sort of a crown on his head with different coloured jewels going across it. He looked like a king."

I wanted to go into more detail, asking her about the colours on this crown but we just sat there in silence finishing off our lunch.

I felt that what happened yesterday was real. What Leigh said to me this morning, and what she said to me just now - no one else could have known this. It couldn't have been a coincidence.

I changed the subject and asked her how the house move was going. She was getting a place with her boyfriend, it was getting serious now. They were moving in together into a penthouse apartment. It was a top-floor apartment with an outdoor garden and balcony, with views right across the whole of Redgrand. It wasn't as tall as the hospital, but it did make part of the Redgrand skyline.

"I'll never move again," she said. "It nearly killed me, don't ever move Az. Stay where you are, you won't cope with the stress."

I wanted to tell her the stress I was feeling right now, but I didn't. I couldn't. I needed more proof before I told anyone about this, even Leigh.

"But we're all settled in now, nice and cosy. I'm just waiting on my garden furniture to be delivered then I'm kind of all moved in."

"House warming party?" I asked.

"Oh aye," she said as she munched off a piece of sausage from her fork.

Her boyfriend was a theatre manager, and he would often get us free or cheap tickets for shows. We loved nothing more than to sit in the back row of the theatre for free, watching whatever we could. We would then proceed to critique the show we had just watched as if it was us that had directed it or had starred in it, not that we were actors or anything, that wasn't our thing. We just loved to bitch and laugh at something in the show, and to also give credit when credit was due.

Leigh finished off her full English breakfast and proceeded to pull out a tube of Pringles from her oversized handbag.

"Pring?" She said as she flicked off the lid with her thumb and offered them out to me.

"No, thanks," I said.

"No Pringles for this boy? Oh, Pringle-Boy doesn't want any, hey? Poor Pringle-boy you don't know what you're missing." She popped four pringles in her mouth at the same time.

My iPad beeped telling me my break was over and having heard this we had 3 minutes to click onto the next job.

Dept: Ward 29

Sender: Sister Lana

Requirement: Transfer the patient to the chemo unit.

I clicked accept.

"Ward 29," I said.

"I'll walk with you," she said as she clicked the lid back on her Pringles and took the last swig of her tea. "I just need to nip to the toilet, wait on."

I waited outside the ladies' toilets; two young student nurses walked past me, they both looked at me and went into a quick walk whilst giggling. I don't know if they were laughing at me because I was standing outside the ladies' toilets or because perhaps one of them fancied me. Either way, I went red with embarrassment and started to move on. Leigh soon caught up with me.

"Hey you've still got it, pal," she said. "Those two student nurses were all over you."

"Ooh did you see his eyes," she mimicked them. "I like an older man," she continued to mock flying straight into her unmistakable belly laugh. We laughed our way back to the ward.

If we were at my house or vice versa and we went into what we call belly laughs, that was it. We would not be able to stop laughing. It could go on for hours. At times, I have been in pain and been unable to breathe because of the laughter. We have this chemistry that only me and Leigh understand. Other people would think we were completely bonkers, and they would be right. As soon as we entered the ward the laughter stopped. We were professional. Leigh went to her locker room, and I went to the nurse's station to look for Sister Lana.

"Hi, Aaron," she said. "There's a little girl in the waiting room with her mum, she only looks about five bless her. Someone's directed her here to Ward 29 for her chemotherapy. She's not going to get it here. Be a darling Aaron, would you take them to the chemo unit?"

"Sure thing," I said as I gave her a wink and a smile.

I walked around the corner towards the waiting room and sat out of view behind the fake plastic plants was this thin, emaciated child. She looked to be about three years old, but you could tell she was older. She had no hair, and her skin was so pale you could see the veins in her head. She had a nasogastric tube fastened to her pale skin on the right side of her face.

My heart broke as I saw her with knee-high white socks and ruby red Mary-Jane shoes, swinging her legs from the plastic bucket chair in the waiting room. She was looking around and taking in her new surroundings. Her mum was sitting next to her reading one of the hospital leaflets. She looked tired and worn, and you could see the worry, stress, and sleepless nights she's had all over her face.

"Hello," I said as I approached her. "My name's Aaron, would you like me to get you a taxi to the chemotherapy unit?"

She looked up and gave me the biggest smile, "Taxi?" she said. And before I could say anything else, Sister Lana beat me to it and whizzed around the corner with a wheelchair.

"Come on, hop into Aaron's Taxi, he doesn't charge much. If you're good, he likes to give rides for free!"

Her mum broke a smile, and the little girl jumped into the over-sized adult wheelchair, she looked so lost sat in the middle of the chair. She placed her doll next to her and said, "Come on - we go adventure."

"What's your name then?" I asked.

"Caroline" she replied.

I quickly broke out into song, singing the lyrics to Sweet Caroline.

"That's the only part I know," I said to her mum.

"Same here," she said.

"And what do they call your doll?"

"Today she's called Jane".

"Don't ask?" her mum said as soon as Caroline stopped speaking.

"First time at Redgrand Hospital then?" I said to the mother.

"Yeah, the chemo unit at SR has closed due to an outbreak, some kind of infection. It's taken us two hours to get here, but she needs her treatment. I'd travel twenty four hours if I had to."

I'd do the same if it was my own kid.

We got to the lifts. "Halfway there," I said, as the mum started patting her pockets and panic struck across her face.

"Oh no," she said in a high-pitched voice. "I've left my purse on the chairs in the waiting room."

"Don't worry, it will still be there. I'm sure. Do you want me to go get it for you?"

"No no", she said. "It's my fault, I'll run back and get it."

She knelt and lowered herself to Caroline's level, "Are you ok waiting here with..." She looked up at me as if to read my name badge.

"Aaron," I said.

"With Aaron?" She continued, "While mummy goes back to fetch her purse?"

"It's ok, Mummy," she said.

"I'll be as quick as I can. I'm so sorry!" She apologised to me and off she flew down the corridor.

My mini-iPad pinged and made the noise. It was an urgent job, but it was at the other end of the hospital, and I knew Shep would pick it up. The little girl saw my iPad and held her hands out.

"Peppa Pig," she squealed, reaching out as if she thought she would be able to watch Peppa Pig from it.

"No, not on this one I'm afraid," I said as I lowered myself to her level and showed her my screen. "This iPad tells my taxi where to go next, you see." I pointed out the lists of jobs waiting to be accepted by porters, and as I showed it to her, Shep picked up the urgent call. The next job was from the Chemo Unit. As I was heading there, I would be taking that next job.

"Do you see that blue box there?" I showed her my screen and said, "That's where I'm going next. Do you want to click it?"

She smiled. She raised her right hand, and I took hold of it to guide her to the correct button on the screen. I didn't want her to click one of the other jobs, which would have meant me having to walk right to the other side of the hospital. The moment my skin made a connection with hers, BOOM.

The wave of energy that overcame me was unexpected. I had experienced this feeling before. All of my senses became activated. The vibrations that went through my chest wall were, again, like being stood in front of the most prominent speaker in a festival. Only this time, my eyes were open. I was awake, and so was the little girl.

She looked at me in awe and wonderment. I looked into her eyes, and I could see the pain and torment she was going through. Her body glowed with an aura around it. I don't know if anyone else could see it, but I could. She had beautiful colours swirling around her. I could still see her physical body, but built in was this mist-like, extra, see-through reality layered on top. I looked more closely at the colours swirling and misting around her body. Then I saw it. A darkness that I can only describe as negative energy. It was around her kidneys like dark smoke choking the life out of them. The little girl, Caroline, was transfixed on me; she could not take her eyes off me.

I looked at my hands, arms, and chest, my entire body was emanating a luminous glow of gold and yellow, just like in the dream. Precisely as Leigh had described. At that moment, I don't know how, and I don't know why, but I knew I could remove the negative energy swirling around on either side of her kidneys. The gloomy swirls of smoke began to move from either side of her kidneys. It rose above the areas where her kidneys would be, met in the middle, and joined as one. Then it continued up her chest wall and descended her right arm. Onto her hand and then the tips of her fingers. It transferred itself into me. As it exited Caroline, and entered into my hand, it sparkled refracting light around us like reflections from a moonlit ocean. As soon as the energy was inside me, I pulled away. The little girl was still looking at me, mesmerised. I looked at my hand. I was still glowing like a luminous light bulb.

"iLUMiNO," she said in an excited tone, pointing at me and giving me the biggest happiest smile that I had seen in a long time.

"iLUMiNO, iLUMiNO, iLUMiNO," she repeated, as her bottom was jumping up and down in the oversized wheelchair with excitement. She then went into giggles of laughter and sat her doll beside her who had fallen to one side.

I smiled at her. The luminous gold glow that I'd had was gone. I knew something else was gone as well. I couldn't say for sure, but right there, right then, as soon as we broke contact, I knew she was now cancer-free.

Just then, her mum came around the corner, a little out of breath with her purse in her hand.

"You got it," I said knowing, of course, she had, as I could see it clutched so tight her fingernails were digging into the leather.

"Yeah," she said, "the ward Sister found it and put it in a safe place for me, thankfully". I pressed the button for the lift, and the doors opened. Dr Shuster came flying out of the lift doors not giving them time to open fully. He brushed my shoulder with his and nearly knocked me over.

"He wanted out," I said. "Obviously attending an emergency," I said to the mum as we entered the lift.

A few seconds passed as we stood there in silence and Caroline sat in her wheelchair playing with her doll.

I looked over at the mum and said, "You know?" Then I paused to create the illusion I was contemplating what to say next, "While you're here at a different hospital, why don't you ask the new doctors for a progression report. You know, to see how's she's doing, see if they want to run any more tests or something?"

"You know, I might just do that."

Caroline smiled at me, a huge smile. She knew.

SIX
Graveyard Shift

Nearly a week has passed since I met the little girl, Caroline, and her Mum at work. Since then, I've had this internal smile on my face. I've tried to keep myself busy, keeping my mind active, and trying not to think about what happened outside the hospital lifts. It hasn't been easy, but I've managed. I've worked two more long day shifts, met up with friends, gone food shopping. I managed to get some gardening done and even managed to squeeze in a meal out with Lottie.

Occasionally, I'd get a text message from Lottie, "Fancy a curry night?"

Lottie was a spur of the moment kind of girl. No planning, or putting a date in our diary, if she wanted a curry that evening, she would have one. If I was available, I'd always say yes. Then we would arrange when, where and what time to meet. If I was working or had other plans, I'd see Lottie on my Facebook feed. I would scroll up the newsfeed that evening, then Lottie would pop up. Instead of posting a selfie with me, it would be with somebody else. What Lottie wanted, Lottie got. She worked hard and rarely did anything for herself. She was a family-orientated person, devoted to her family and her husband. Still, on the odd occasion, she would think to herself, 'it's my turn now', and treat herself to a meal. Mainly her treats were food with friends, but that was Lottie.

The noise of the letterbox springing back, metal against metal, woke me up with a jolt. I had slept in, unless the postman was early. I checked the time on my iPhone. It was 11:11 am. I could not remember the last time I slept in until this late hour on a morning. It took me a good ten minutes to gather up enough energy to get out of bed, and even then, I felt I could have rolled over and gone back to sleep.

Instead, I stretched out, yawned, and sat on the edge of the bed. Scraped my hair back out of my eyes and ruffled it back itching my head at the same time. I didn't even bother with my dressing gown, I just headed downstairs in my boxer shorts and went straight to the front door. Two letters sat on the mat. One in a brown recycled envelope which didn't have my address on it and in bold type it read 'to the homeowner'. I didn't even open it, and I took it straight to the kitchen's recycling bin. The other was a white envelope, the kind of envelope that resembled a birthday or Christmas card. I switched the kettle on in the kitchen and sat in my chair. It wasn't my birthday, and I had no known reason for any cards to be sent to me. The envelope was handwritten, and I instantly recognised the handwriting. I opened the envelope.

'Home Sweet Home', it read in big, bold letters across the top of the card. It was an invitation.

"You are invited to Leigh & Adam's Housewarming Party."

In smaller italics, it read, "Don't bring us a gift, bring your favourite drink instead."

It was for next Friday. I looked at my calendar on the fridge to check. I was available. I couldn't believe she hadn't told me to pencil in the date. As the kettle boiled, I sent her a text with my RSVP, 'Try keeping me away, looking forward to it!'

Within an instant, she replied with an emoji thumbs up and a red love heart.

Today was my day off from work, and I had a run of three long day shifts starting the following day. I had made a mental list the night before of all the things that I needed to do on my last day off... Laundry, post office, and a visit to Mum & Dad's. I always paid a visit to my parents on the last day of every month.

I never worked on the last day of the month. I always made sure that I hadn't got any shifts booked in at work. Even the boss knew not to ask me to work any extra on those days, even if they were short-staffed, as he knew my priority was Mum & Dad's on the last day of the month.

Mum and Dad were childhood sweethearts. They met at school and were raised in good, stable, loving families. Both of them came from homes where they were the only child, no other siblings in their life. Mum says she always wanted a brother to pick on, and dad used to say the same, about a sister. They lived just across the street from each other, and they grew up as best friends. Sleepovers, fights, birthday parties. They went to the same high school, and as they grew up together, they became soul mates. Everyone knew they were destined for each other. As they got older, they did eventually fall in love. They were married by the time my Mum was twenty one. Dad was only nineteen, and he was so proud that he was going to be a dad.

Being an only child means that I am the only one who can tend to their grave. All four of my grandparents died when I was relatively young.

Mum and Dad died in a car accident on my 21st birthday. I still get mad and angry at them for leaving me so early on in my life. My 21st birthday was supposed to be a lovely afternoon in the garden. Mum had bought a gazebo and decorated it with balloons and banners saying '21 Today'. Dad got the BBQ out, and I was looking forward to having a lovely afternoon with my Mum and Dad, and a few of my friends.

The day before, I'd spotted a birthday cake with a picture printed on the icing of me as a toddler. It was a photograph of me sitting on the potty with a cheeky grin on my face. I never said anything. I thought I'd act surprised and embarrassed for the sake of my folks.

I'd got some old high school friends coming over, mainly Barkley, Brenda, Leigh, and Penelope. Lottie was coming over too, and I was looking forward to having a drink and enjoying my friends' company. It was ten am, and I was still in my room. The party was to begin at twelve midday.

Mum shouted upstairs to me, "Aaron we're just popping out, we will be 30 mins or so, stay out of the garden, it's a surprise!"

I didn't know at the time, but they had gone to collect a second-hand car they had bought for me as a surprise for my 21st birthday. I thought it was strange that they both left the house in Mum's red Fiat Punto. Dad was always the driver if they went out together. Unbeknownst to me, when they had gone to collect the surprise birthday car, Mum was driving Dad there to complete the sale, and Dad would drive my present home. I saw some red ribbon and a bow on the kitchen worktop, but I just thought it was part of the decorations. It was a blue Ford Escort.

I remember seeing the pictures in the local newspaper of the accident. 'Motorway carnage,' the headlines read. Mum's red Fiat Punto was halfway into the blue Ford Escort that dad was driving. The photos made it look like someone had spliced two cars together. Both Mum and Dad were pronounced dead at the scene.

A Mr Terry Stamp was selling the car. He wasn't able to drive any longer due to health issues. The vehicle had not moved for eight months. He only lived ten minutes away from our house. According to the accident report, the calliper on the brakes had seized. Dad must have applied the brakes at some point when he was driving it home, and that was it, they seized. Mum was behind him in her car, and she went straight into the back of him. Neither of them stood a chance.

Thursday 31st July 1997 wasn't my 21st birthday. It was the day I lost my world.

The accident happened on the last day of July. The funeral service on the last day of August. Since then, and every month since, I have tended to their grave on the last day of every month. I have come to terms with my loss, but it was a long grieving process. It was nearly a decade before I was able to come off the medication. I had an abundance of love through the whole ordeal from my friends. Leigh was there for me when I was rock bottom, as were Barkley, and Lottie.

I know of the saying 'pushing up daisies'. Well, this was so true of my Mum and Dad's grave. Every month the same weed would appear in the same spot, and every month I would pull it out. I'd give the grave a clean down, remove the old dead flowers and replace them with fresh ones. This time though, I came prepared. I'd bought some weed killer during my last shopping spree. It's only taken me twenty three years to realise that I'd not been taking the weeds out by the roots. By now, the white gravel had turned green with moss and algae. Once upon a time, I would be able to rake the stones, and as they turned over, it would reveal the whiteness of the rocks again. Those days were long gone, the gravel now looked like it was supposed to be green. I had thought about replacing it, but it's not easy on a pushbike.

I never did get a car after Mum and Dad's car accident.

As I tended to the grave, I sat there like I have done many times before. I spoke to my parents. They always listened when they were alive, and I have carried on telling them about my life. I'd often go with loads of stuff to tell them. Other times, I preferred to sit there in solitude listening to the wildlife and the trees in the breeze around the graveyard.

I arrived at the grave at 1 pm, much later than usual. I would typically arrive at 10 am and I'd see Mrs Douglas, who lost her husband five years ago. She would always be sitting on a bench in front of her husband's gravestone. Sometimes, I would sit with her and talk. At the very least, I would give her a nod or a friendly hello. She would probably be wondering where I was today. I started pulling weeds up and spraying the weed killer. A sudden urge came over me, I sat the weed killer down and cried. I'd not wept at my parents' grave for years. My head was a total mess, something was happening to me, and I had no one to talk to

about it. I took a deep sigh and a long pause. It was as if I was going to
tell them something so big, and I hesitated as if I was going to be scared
of the response. I eventually told them about Metatron in my dream
and of floating outside the tent. I told them about Leigh and what she
saw, and about the little girl at the hospital.

I started thinking back to being outside the lift area at the hospital
with Caroline. I could visualise myself with this golden aura around my
body, and this little girl looking at me in wonderment.

"What was happening to me?" I asked Mum and Dad.

Silence fell, and I carried on cleaning the grave, tears streaming
down my face. I placed some fresh flowers in the marble vase that
formed part of the headstone.

"I'll see you next month," I said and slowly picked up my bike. I
walked with it to the gates at the graveyard. Just as I was about to leave,
I saw Mrs Douglas getting out of her car in the small car park. I dried
off my face and waited to greet her. She was in her eighties and still driving, an achievement in its own right. She saw me waiting, and her slow
walk picked up the pace.

"Hello, my love," she said as she pulled off her grey knitted hat with
a half-finished pom pom on top. It was the middle of summer, yet she
still wore the same hat every time I saw her.

"Hi, Mrs Douglas," I said.

"I must have missed you this morning," she said in her sweet soft
old lady voice.

"Yeah," I said, shifting my weight to my other foot nervously and
holding onto my bike as if someone was going to steal it. "I had a dentist
appointment this morning," I lied. I didn't want her to think, or know,
that I had overslept.

She looked at me as if she could tell I wasn't telling the truth.
"Ah, the dreaded dentist," she said. "At least I don't have that worry
anymore," and she snapped her teeth shut to make a chomping noise.
"Well, not unless this set breaks, I don't."

"I'm surprised to see you here this afternoon too," I said.

"Oh, my darling, I come here every day, twice a day, and have done for the last five years. You see when my George was dying of cancer, I said to him 'George, you might be leaving me soon, but I am not leaving you. I will still come and see you every day, and I will be with you until I can't any longer. When that time comes, then I will probably be ready to come and join you anyway.'" She pulled out a white flask with red roses on it, "I come here and have a cuppa in the afternoon with my George, come rain or shine I am here."

Listening to her tell me this made me feel guilty about my once-a-month ritual. It hardly felt enough compared to her twice-daily visits.

"Anyway, today we are celebrating. I've got a tot of whisky in my tea, and I'm going to celebrate the good news with my George."

I looked over at her car parked up in the car park.

"Oh, don't worry about that dear," she said. "I nearly always have something to celebrate! The amount of whisky I put in here wouldn't fit in a chocolate liqueur. I've been celebrating with a tot of whisky in this flask for years love. But..." She smiled and looked at the sky. "But today someone was listening, and this one is a true celebration."

"Go on then," I said. "Share the good news!"

"My great-granddaughter has been given the all-clear for cancer," she said as she handed me the flask and pulled out of her bag a small hand-sized photo album, she flicked through towards the last page and showed me the photo.

I did not react; it was like time stood still.

She took the album back out of my hand and held it to her chest. "Caroline, they call her, and she has been given the all-clear of cancer."

SEVEN
Neutral Zone

I don't remember cycling home or getting into bed. Today felt like another dream. The last few weeks of my life felt like a dream. Waking up in my bed, sweating profusely, it felt like I'd awoken from a nightmare, but I couldn't remember having one. Touching my iPhone screen, it lit up at 5 pm. I never sleep in the afternoon. I wasn't well. I was in shock.

Going downstairs and heading straight to the fridge, my bike left in a heap on the living room floor, I grabbed a chilled bottle of water and drank it all without even taking a breath. Closing the fridge door slowly and gently as my mind raced, I leaned onto it resting my head on my arm. I just wanted all of this to go away. This couldn't possibly be happening to me. I ruffled my hair back out of my eyes and walked into the living room, picking my bike up from the floor and standing it against the staircase.

Sitting in my living room oversized leather armchair, I stared into space. I just sat in silence. Eventually, I could feel my eyes and the inside of my nose getting wet. I stared at the photograph on top of my bookcase of my parents taken on their wedding day.

Mum with her soft skin and glowing eyes which matched the whiteness of her dress. My dad with his smart brown suit and white flower buttonhole. Dad was holding Mum's hand with the emphasis on their hands, showing off their wedding rings to the camera. My bottom lip started to quiver as the wetness in my eyes began to pool. One tear ran down the left side of my face. I closed my eyes, and I imagined my mother wiping it away. It made me smile. I know it was just my imagination, but it always felt so real when I imagined her. Whenever I needed her, I would imagine her, and she would appear. She never spoke to me. I didn't need her to, just knowing that I could still feel her love was enough.

"What's happening to me, Mum?" My voice broke and cracked.

I sniffled my running nose and wiped my tears away. I sat eyes red and puffy, my nose snotty and bunged up. I just wanted to cry out so loud. I felt alone. I felt afraid. I was worried that these past events were real, or that I was losing my mind. Both options were not good. For more than half of my life, I have felt alone, but this was new. This was very new to me. I was alone, and I couldn't tell anyone about this, not even Leigh, not Lottie, and certainly not Barkley. For the first time, I had no one to talk things over.

"Mum, I need you!" I sobbed. "I need you."

I hadn't cried like this in a long time. It was as if all the grief that I had gone through twenty years ago was back. Like it had never gone. It felt as raw now as it did then. I had done so well.

I cradled my head in my hands. I needed a hanky to wipe my eyes and my nose. Lifting my head slowly, I was just about to lean forward to the side table and grab a tissue from the box. And there, floating right in front of my face was a tissue. It had the same golden glow around it that I had come to recognise.

I just stared at in awe. I wasn't shocked, nor was I scared; I was mesmerised. Slowly, I tilted my head to the side, scrutinising this tissue floating right before me.

Shrugging my shoulders as if this was an everyday occurrence, I tentatively reached out with my right arm to take it.

My hand, arm, and entire body glowed too, the same as the tissue. The golden waves were slowly emitting outwards in sync with the tissue. I recognised the feeling of my cells being alive; activated. I took hold of the tissue, and the golden aura surrounding myself and the tissue became one.

I blew my nose using the tissue just in time before a drop of mucus fell.

I looked at my hands with the golden colours swirling out of my skin, and then looked at my arms, and then my chest, and my entire body. I realised I was wearing the colour purple and gold; the glow illuminated my skin. Still, I wasn't scared, frightened, or even freaked out. I was so calm and collected. I felt peaceful. Rising slowly from the oversized armchair, I headed towards my full-length mirror next to the front door. I would often use this mirror to check and make sure my hair and clothes looked decent before leaving the house. It was still daylight outside, yet as I moved around the room the golden glow emanating from my body was casting shadows, like a candle in the night. I looked into the mirror, and I knew what I was going to see. I was right, the reflection in the mirror was exactly the same as in my dream. My hair was golden brown, and longer, and flicked out at the sides. My nose was thinner just like it was in the dream. I was wearing the same dark robe, its purple and gold energy pulsating up and down to a point in the gold woven fabric. My shoes were golden and looked like they were alive, like they were plugged into an electrical socket.

A golden cloak fell from my right shoulder, pinned by a golden badge, the same one that Metatron wore in my dream. Atop my head was a crown with seven jewels of such beauty, each with a life-source inside. Reaching to my ear, both my piercings had gone. I looked at myself in the mirror. I took a step back and started to shake my head in disbelief. The light emanating from my body filled the room with embers of golden light flickering in all directions. I could feel the anxiety inside building up. Still, I was soon relaxed when a familiar voice spoke.

"Relax, Aaron, do not be afraid." It was Metatron, and his voice filled the room. I could not tell if he was behind me or beside me. His voice was loud and transparent like a surround sound system charging into my head, so endearing and loving. Hearing Metatron prompted me to turn around, but he was not there.

At that moment, my living room began to disappear. I could see the living room begin to change into different colours again, like looking at the bottom of a billion empty bottles. The colours of the round spherical pieces of glass began to change to white. I quickly glanced over at my clock on the fireplace. 5:15 pm. Within seconds, it became pixelated and turned white like the rest of the room. I felt like I had been transported somewhere else. All I could see was white. It reminded me of The Matrix movie when Neo was in the 'white room', a construct written by a computer programmer. Yet, I hadn't moved. It didn't feel like I had moved anywhere. It felt like my surroundings had moved, not me. I looked at my hands, arms, body, and feet, I was still wearing the purple robe and golden shoes and cape. I felt my head, and the crown of jewels was still there.

"This is the neutral zone," Metatron said from a distance behind me. This time I could hear his voice from the direction he was coming. He walked closer to me, and his voice got louder. I turned around, and there he was.

"You now have access to the 'neutral zone' whenever you like. Time is of no time here. This you can call your safe zone, your neutral zone, whatever you want to call it. It is where you can come and take stock and ask questions. The neutral zone does not have all the answers for you, but it will help you to achieve solutions you are seeking. Earth time will stand still when you visit here. Think of it like this. You are a character in a book or a TV show, and you have the power to stop the narrative or pause the tv show. As the reader or character of the book or tv show, you can take time out to understand the plot. Here you can ask for guidance, and then you can decide which way the plot or the story continues.

"So, I can ask questions?"

"Yes, you have so many questions already, many of which I have already told you the answer to. But I will share them again."

It was as if he could read my mind because I did not ask any questions; he knew what I wanted to know.

"Yes, this is happening to you," he said. "You are not experiencing a hallucination or a dream. This is happening to you right now. You are on a new spiritual and physical aspect of your current life. The changes are all unusual to you because you are still with blood, or in other words, you have a physical body; flesh and blood.

"Because you still have this physical shape, the changes you are experiencing will feel extraordinary and appear non-human. The closest thing I can relate to is in your popular culture; you have fictional heroes with super human powers. Aaron Abbey, this is you, but it's not imaginary or fictitious. It is real. You are not fiction; you are real. You have new abilities, some of which you have already worked out for yourself, but you are so much more than skills and powers. For the first time in man's timeline, there is a 'physical body', a physical body that has similar abilities as us higher beings. The aforementioned can only become a benefit for the human race, for the planet earth and the cosmos."

At this point, I was overwhelmed by what Metatron was saying to me. "I'm just a porter, I'm no one special." I contemplated how this would affect my life. "Not just my life, but my friends, my work, how can I exist if I am like this? What will happen to me? Aaron, the nice guy with the bobble end nose and short messy hair and both ears pierced. What about my life?"

"This is your life," Metatron calmly replied. "Your life can be however you choose it. The options are endless, and the decision you make will be the right one. You can live your life fully as your higher self. Or at the other end of the spectrum, you could block out your higher self and never see your higher self, or me, again. And in between those two alternatives are more than a billion variables. You just have to choose which path to take, or maybe the course may choose you. Either way, it will be the right choice."

"Right ok," I said, not quite sure what else to say. "Well, for a start..." I looked at my robe and golden light-up shoes, "If this is going to happen, then this robe has got to go." Instantly, and as quick as I said it, the robe, cloak, and shoes disappeared, and I was naked.

Strangely, I did not feel the need to cover myself. I wasn't embarrassed or ashamed of my naked body. I looked down and took a look at my higher self... naked. Impressed with my examination down below, I looked at Metatron, "I can live with that."

"Perhaps though," Metatron replied, "The people in your current timeline will not be so accepting of your current lack of attire."

"Agreed."

I looked up as if trying to remember a designed costume from a comic book or movie. Instantly, I was wearing a purple and gold skintight suit, covering my face and eyes. It resembled a Spiderman costume. I shook my head, scratching at my eyes, "How on earth does he see out of this thing!"

I put my hand on my chin, poised in thought. Batman came to mind, I used to watch the animated cartoon as a child. In an instant, I was wearing a similar-looking Batman costume, still in the colours of purple and gold. I shook my head as Metatron looked on with no real expression on his face. I thought of the superman mug that Leigh had bought me. The purple and gold batman costume turned into a purple and gold Superman costume.

"I'm no good at this!" I said to Metatron, standing there in the white room dressed in a purple superman costume.

"Close your eyes," he said, "Let the 'neutral zone' choose for you."

"Pardon?"

"Close your eyes and relax."

I sighed a deep breath and reluctantly closed my eyes. A small moment passed.

"Now open them."

I looked down and I was wearing golden knee-high boots. The boots were like the original shoes, with golden waves starting from the middle and working their way out creating an aura. The purple Superman costume was still present, but it was like a purple wetsuit, and without underwear on the outside.

The 'S' symbol on the chest was gone and in its place were seven coloured stones spaced out in a circle evenly from the centre of my chest. They were the same colours as those on the crown, but now the crown had gone. The cape was no longer hanging from one shoulder. It was now symmetrical, hanging from both shoulders held in place by two gold badges in the shape of Metatron's Cube on each shoulder. The cape was golden with purple lines of thread woven into the golden material, starting across my back and forming at a point at the bottom. The front had the same pattern, but in gold thread. It began from my shoulders and travelled downwards to a point meeting the red jewel at my navel. The golden energy running down the thread was like an electrical current.

"I can make this work," I said. I spun around as if I was with Leigh in a shop dressing room, pulling back the curtain and showing off a new designer suit.

I looked good, and I felt good. I could see the definition in my body. I didn't feel pretentious, it wasn't as if I wanted to show it off, but I did feel proud.

"This is more me, yeah I like it."

Metatron just stared at me; his face did not move, the only visible thing that was moving was the energy surrounding him, his aura.

"What?" I said, looking directly at Metatron.

He said nothing, just continued to stare into me, not one facial muscle, if he had any, moved.

"Ok, so you said I have many powers, some of which I have already found out for myself," I thought for a moment.

"So, there's the little girl with cancer, I healed her, then there's the floating tissue... So I can manipulate objects and control them? Right?"

Metatron nodded.

"Fly, yes, I was in the air at the campsite. I can fly?"

Metatron nodded again.

"Oh my god, I don't have to ride my bike to work ever again!" I smiled to myself.

I continued to think of the other experiences I'd had, "Oh yes, what about my zoom vision... But I felt like I was there, when Leigh saw me, my eyes zoomed in, right? To where she was at work?"

"You were there Aaron," Metatron said "You were outside the hospital. Your eyes did not zoom in; you can project your physical body anywhere on the earth's plane. If you are happy and feel safe where your physical body is projecting, then the physical body can join you."

"So I can go anywhere in the world?"

Metatron nodded.

"Anywhere?" I said excitedly.

I had never left England. I was going to enjoy this.

"Anything else?" I said, rubbing my hands together as if I had just won the lottery.

"You can heal, you already know that, but you can also heal yourself. Beware, you are not immune to injury, your body is of flesh and blood. You will still experience pain, but you can heal on a transient level. The extent of the damage will impact the speed of your healing. If you do suffer pain, you will learn to send that negative energy out of your body. The earth will pick this up and digest it."

"Can I make myself invisible?"

"Not in the way that you think of invisibility. It depends upon your resonance or your frequency. These factors impact whether people can see you or not. You have the potential to be invisible. Still, there will be some element of your presence. If you lower your resonance, it may be possible, but not guaranteed. They may see your aura or the gold light that you emit."

"Aaron, you are also able to manifest through physical matter."

"What? I can what?"

"You can change your frequency within this world, meaning you can pass through physical matter. You have a lot of new experiences to come your way. Get to know yourself, Aaron Abbey. The world is waiting for a positive change. Be that change."

And with that, he was gone, his voice reverberating as if I was in a cave.

'Be that change', I liked that.

The whiteness of the room began to look pixelated, and one by one, it looked like the pixels were turning off, but it was the living room coming back. Within seconds I was back in my living room, and the clock on the fireplace still read 5:15 pm. I had been with Metatron for what felt like ten minutes. He was right, time did not move in the neutral zone.

EIGHT
Taking Flight

It was Friday at 5 am, and my alarm kicked in, waking me abruptly. I must have gone straight to bed after my visit from Metatron yesterday evening because I don't have any memory from then.

Quickly, I started getting ready in the bathroom; throwing some water onto my face and trying to brush my teeth at the same time. I was trying to think if I had prepared my sandwich for lunch today at work. I spat out the toothpaste and took a swig of mouthwash. Taking a glance at myself in the mirror, I ruffled my hair back.

As I entered the kitchen, I could see a light that I did not recognise. The fridge door was wide open. I looked at the milk in the carton and I could see it had curdled. I couldn't see anything that I'd prepared for lunch.

Rushing around trying to get ready, I just thought to myself that I'd buy something from the canteen. I was just about to get my bike out of the shed when I remembered what Metatron had said about projecting myself to a place and then allowing myself to transport to it.

My bike was half in and half out of the shed. I stood still and froze.

I imagined being at the bicycle shelter at work. I could see in my memory, in my mind's eye, the bike shelter. I imagined being there. Slowly, and not feeling scared or freaked out, I could see that my body had started to light up in golden colours. Just like before, I felt my eyes zooming in like a video camera, and in what felt like a split second, there I was outside the bike shelter. I could see the bike stand. I could feel a different breeze, and at the same time, I was aware that I was still in my back garden. My bike in my hands with the back wheel still inside the shed. I was aware I was in two places at once. Looking around the car park, the bike shelter was deserted, not a soul in sight. I relaxed took a breath in. I started to close my eyes, and I thought to myself, "Ok, I'll allow myself to be there."

As soon as I conceived that thought, and before I closed my eyes, or even processed what may happen, the bicycle stand outside the hospital felt like it was enfolding me. It felt as if I was looking through a fisheye lens, my vision was distorted and curving around me.

Like a train going past, it whooshed and then it popped from fisheye vision to a photograph becoming 3D. And there I was, standing outside the hospital, mountain bike in hand. I could see the golden embers of light fading away from my body. Looking around to see if anyone was about, I was shocked, scared, nervous, and excited at the same time. I locked up my bike. My hands were shaking with excitement. Composing myself, and taking in deep breaths, I headed towards the automatic doors at the hospital. Jeanette was sat at the reception desk and gave me a warm welcome,

"You're early," she said with a smile. I looked at the clock on the wall behind her, she was right. I was fifteen minutes early. But I would be, I didn't cycle there.

"So I am!"

"Are you ok? Jeanette said. "You have a red line down one side of your face."

"I'm ok, I guess." I used the glass screen between us to check my reflection.

She was right, I could see I had a red line down my face.

Realising I had only been awake ten minutes, and it was the indent from the pillow left on my face, I said, "I'm ok. It will fade soon. See you later!" And I carried on through the corridors heading towards the lift.

My shift at work was a busy one. I knew it would be as there were seven ambulances out front. I managed to get a late lunch break. The lovely girl behind the counter who looked young enough to be on work experience made me a fresh sandwich without any butter on it.

Leigh wasn't working today, but I was too busy to stop and chat even if she was. Each job I clicked on using the iPad, I had a fleeting 'shall I or shall I not' moment. I had a cheeky smile on my face knowing I could teleport there or materialise, or whatever it was that I had managed to do this morning. I didn't, obviously. People would scream if all of a sudden I popped up out of thin air in front of them.

I felt like the day had gone quickly. I didn't take time to stop and chat as I usually would. The workload was non-stop, and I thought I had to get to the next job as soon as possible. Finally, my shift was finishing, so I began to make my way towards the porters' changing area. I logged out of the iPad, leaving it on its docking station. I changed out of my uniform and headed out, checking my pockets to make sure I had my iPhone and the key for my bike chain. Turning right from one of the long corridors to the next, I bumped into Brandon. Brandon was one of the new hospital security guards. He was in his late teens and did not look like he could secure anything. His uniform looked far too big for him. He didn't look like a typical security guard, he was skinny with a pale complexion. If I were to place him in a stereotypical job, I would have him sit at a desk writing a computer programme. He was a friendly kid, but that's what he was to me, still a kid.

"Whoa, sorry Brandon," I said as we seemed to do the tango on the corridor.

"No, don't be," he said. "I was coming up to hopefully catch you before you left."

"Everything ok?"

"Aaron," he said, "You're not going to believe this, but you're famous."

"I'm what?"

"You're famous. Well kind of anyway."

"What do you mean, kind of?"

"Well, you can't see your face so no one can tell it's you, but it must be you because it's your bike being locked up."

I had a terrible feeling I knew where this conversation was heading.

"Here," he said. "Check this out," he pulled out his phone and unlocked it using his facial recognition, flicked at his phone with his thumb until he came to the YouTube app.

"Press play on that," he handed me the phone.

I took the device from his hand and tentatively pressed play.

It was a recording of the security cameras set around the hospital, filmed in the security room. There looked to be more than a hundred cameras. To the right was one screen which was full size. You could tell it was recorded by hand as the camera is shaking and moving around a lot. Clearly and excitedly, you hear Brandon from behind the camera say, "Watch this guys. Just watch this..."

He moves the camera closer. I could see it was a static camera shot of the bicycle stand. It was in black and white and pixelated. I knew what I was going to see. I remained calm. Brandon looked at my face for my reaction. I could feel his eyes boring into my face to see what response I would deliver. The video continued to play, and the camera started to shake further as Brandon's left-hand reaches for the mouse near the screen. Brandon in the recording clicks the play icon on the television screen.

Nothing happened for the first ten seconds. It was just the bicycle stand in black and white. To the screen's right, a white vertical oval glow appeared from nowhere. The light expanded as the white balance on the security camera tried to adjust. The whiteness nearly encompassed the entire screen like a flashlight going off from a camera.

It took about one and a half seconds. The whiteness faded away. The camera tried to refocus on the bicycle stand, and there I am clear as day looking around. You cannot make out my facial features, but Brandon knows it's me, and I know it's me.

"Wow, is that me? Did I just ping out of nowhere? How did you do that?" I gave him the phone back, "You're in the wrong job Brandon, you need to be in television or special effects."

"I've not messed with the video Aaron. This is what it recorded. That is the actual footage."

"Haha, yeah right! Well, I'm impressed. You really should consider movie effects as a career."

"Aaron, I'm telling you, man, I've not messed with the footage. This is legit."

"Oh, ok I'll go with that then. If you have not messed with the video footage, I would tell your bosses your cameras need checking out. There is some glitch, I mean you don't think I just appeared out of nowhere, do you?"

He didn't answer; he just shrugged his shoulders and said, "I don't know."

"How many views has this YouTube video glitch recording of yours got?" I said, grabbing the phone back out of his hand.

"No way," I said as I glanced at the total views. Over six thousand. Posted eleven hours ago.

"I know," he said. "Nearly seven thousand views. I've never had so many."

I could feel my throat drying up. "Who else has seen this at work?" I asked.

"Just me up to now, but I have logged it as a job for my boss to look at it. Whether he has or not, I don't know."

"Look it's probably a glitch in the system. It's obvious it's a glitch in the system, but Brandon you are going to have to take it down from YouTube."

"Why? No way, I'm getting loads of hits. It's a good video."

"Well, if you want to get sacked then leave it up."I handed the phone back.

"What do you mean get sacked?"

"Information governance, Brandon. You're breaking every rule going."

"Information? What are you on about?"

"Brandon, you can quite clearly see where you are as you film this. You can see the hospital logo on a poster on the wall. You can see all the hospital cameras. Your YouTube channel is your name, 'Brandon James'. If your boss sees this video, it will be instant dismissal I promise you."

I could see the colour from his pale face draining. The vein in his temples began to bulge as he processed the information I'd just told him.

"Crap! I never thought. Oh god, you're right. I'll delete it straight away."

I patronised him and laughed, "I told you you were in the wrong job, best security guard out there!"

I left him standing there on the corridor frantically tapping his screen on his phone.

I made my way to the bicycle shelter, unlocked my bike, and cycled home.

Taking a shower after work was therapeutic, I had the showerhead on the jet which punched the water into my back. I was thinking about my quick journey to work, and I was thanking Metatron in my head for how he had helped me feel relaxed about my new abilities. I know I would have been freaking out otherwise. I had a peaceful new outlook on life. I was also thinking of other places I could visit. Random thoughts were popping in my head. The recording that Brandon had made and the potential number of people who had seen it. Not that any of it mattered, the footage was a second screen recording; it could have been a fake and the quality was low.

I had to be more careful in future.

Towelling down, I sat on the closed toilet seat as I dried in between my toes. I slipped on my dressing gown and looked at myself in the mirror.

"How do I change into the purple and gold guy?" I thought.

I closed my eyes and took a deep, slow breath in, and then out.

At the same time, I was thinking of myself as Mr Purple Man. Before I even opened my eyes, I could feel the energies changing within me, electrical activity pulsating as each cell became alive. I closed my eyes. I could see through my eyelids the brightness and golden colour breaking through. Slowly I opened them, and no longer was I wearing my dressing gown. I was the purple man with a golden cloak, boots, and a golden aura all around the outline of my body. Still in my bathroom, I looked closely at myself in the mirror, checking out my skin, my ears without any piercing and my perfect nose. My eyes were the deepest blue with a purple edge around the iris.

"Is this what Metatron meant? The world is waiting for a positive change. Be that change! Me as Mr Purple Man? Is this what he meant for me?"

I wanted to try this flying thing again. The only experience I had was floating above the camp chair while Barkley was fast asleep. I wanted to see if I could fly properly.

Walking into the back garden, the golden glow coming from my body lit the garden up like a firework. The outside light became activated, whitewashing out the golden glow.

I could see Mr Williams's house next door and his upstairs bedroom light came on. His curtains were still open and the window slightly open on the latch. I didn't want him to see me. I looked up at the dark sky. I didn't know how to fly. I didn't know if it would work. I just imagined being up there in the sky and imagined I was looking down.

With a swoosh, I felt like I was on a reverse roller coaster. I felt like my stomach was in my boots as I flew up into the darkness of the sky.

The feeling of not being governed by gravity was a whole new feeling in itself. It wasn't like the first time when I was floating above the camp chair. I have no other experiences to compare. I can only describe it as being in a diving pool. Still, this description does not come close to the freedom and the agility my body had in the open air. I felt a freedom like never before. I could move in any direction, all I had to do was think, and I would move through the air. Like on a bike you would think about turning left, then you would turn left, it was precisely the same, but I had no vehicle, I was the vehicle.

The view was intoxicating and mesmerising. Weirdly, it was so quiet up in the sky. There was no sound, just the breeze and the sound of my breath as I breathed out. I could see my house, the outside light illuminating my garden which now resembled the size of a piece of Lego. I was feeling elated, euphoric, that all of this was happening to me. The knowledge that I can fly is literally out of this world.

In the sky, I hung there, My golden cape was flapping in the breeze and the golden glow continued to surround my body.

Then I realised, and quickly, that people would see me due to the golden glow around me. I imagined that I must look like a golden lantern in the sky. At this height, approximately one mile above the earth, I assumed I would still be visible with the naked eye. I looked up and went even higher. As I did, I could hear the wind rush between my ears. I listened to the flap of my cape and I noticed that I could see water vapour exiting my mouth, it must have been cold, but I did not feel it. About two miles up, I could still see my house, but more noticeable was my neighbourhood. I could see the shape it took from above with the streetlights lighting up the ground. I could see the hospital in the distance. I wanted to go higher, but I was aware that I might not have any oxygen to breathe. I didn't know my limitations, so I didn't. I wasn't scared, throughout all of this, I was not scared at all. I was embracing every moment.

I could see car headlights lighting up the dark country roads. They looked like snails with headlamps on moving across a winding road. Everything appeared to move slower than usual. At this point I had only travelled upwards and turned around facing a different direction in mid-air, I hadn't journeyed forwards or backwards yet.

I wanted to test my flight and travel. I thought of a place I had never been before and always wanted to go. Brighton, down south, my mum told me of her childhood holidays there. I didn't know which direction to fly in. I supposed if I was higher, and I could see England as an outline like on Google Maps, I would know where to fly. My entire peripheral vision was land. Without thinking about which direction to fly in to get to my destination, I started to drift. It was like a gut feeling. But it was more than that. It was a sense of knowing that this was the right direction, so I went with the flow. I was flying. I was still in a vertical position, moving forward in the direction that I felt was Brighton. I don't know how fast I was flying. Still, it didn't feel fast enough. I began to pick up speed, and as I did, my body began to rotate at an angle. I was becoming vertical, more aerodynamic. I wasn't doing this, it just happened naturally.

I guess I did look like the superheroes from the movies flying through the air, only this time there wasn't any CGI, no wires, and no green screen. It was me, Aaron Abbey, dressed as the purple man with a golden cape, boots, and aura.

The land beneath was moving faster than ever. I did not feel that I was moving fast at all, the wind through my hair and cape, flapping vigorously, was the only indication I had that I was travelling at speed. Within about three minutes, I could see darkness. It was the sea. It was a darkness so black in contrast to the many lights that decorated the shoreline on the promenade.

I'd come to a natural stop. I didn't think it was me making a conscious decision to stop. I just stopped, slowed down, and my body changed from the horizontal position to a vertical position. I felt like

I was sitting down on air. I looked around and thought about going in closer. I didn't make a conscious decision to go in closer. It was like a fleeting thought, and before the thought had even finished processing, I was already moving slowly back to the ground. The white lights were now becoming colours as I got closer. I was about half a mile up in the air, and I could see a multitude of coloured lights from one lamppost to the next. In the distance, I could see the coloured flashing lights of the fairground on the pier; the big wheel lit up like a flashing ten pence piece turning slowly.

Beyond this, I could see street lights and darkness on either side of the street lighting, no buildings, no funfair just countryside on one side and sea on the other. It looked quiet, and hopefully, no one would see me. As soon as I thought it, I was heading in that direction and then I began to descend.

The first thing I noticed was the sound. I could hear the waves crashing onto the rocks. As I got closer, my pupils reacted to the lights as the landscape came towards me. I could smell the sea air, the freshness, the crispness, the beautiful natural air that was Brighton. I landed gracefully as if I had been doing this all my life. Not a soul in sight, I was alone. I took a few steps and leaned on a railing overlooking the beach. The wind was blowing my hair calmly. The sea was lapping at the shore in cosmic rhythm. I looked at my hands; there was the faint glow of gold surrounding me. I realised I was dressed as the Purple Man. I couldn't walk into town dressed like this.

As I thought it, the gold embers dissipated from my hand as did the purple sleeves. Within seconds,

I was standing there leaning on the railing barefooted in my dressing gown. I was instantly freezing. I had to arch my feet and curl my toes inwards to prevent my feet from taking on the cold floor. I could feel the breeze fly straight up my gown, in-between my legs. Embarrassed and freezing, I must have looked like an escaped confused patient from the local hospital.

I could hear a dog barking and a male voice shouting, "Jimmy, Jimmy, here boy!" from a distance. The sound of the dog barking was getting closer, as was the male voice. I did not want him to see me barely naked.

No sooner had I thought about it, I already had the golden glow surrounding my body, and I was wearing the purple suit again.

The dog was in my vision, I could see him running towards me, barking with every leap. I wasn't scared, neither was the dog. He ran right up and sat right in front of me, offering me his paw. His barking was an excited bark. I think he could feel the energy. I could feel his life; it was unconditional love and obedience. I patted his head, and he bowed over. I swear he could understand that I didn't want his owner to see me, and so he turned and ran off.

I could hear his owner saying, "Good boy, Jimmy. Good boy."

I looked up at the sky. The moon was bright and reflected the sea in a line on the horizon. My feet left the ground, and I was high above the promenade again. It was a fleeting visit, but I was pleased I had made it. Next time, I would come prepared.

I went higher and higher. The silence fell upon me as the landmass grew darker. Home. I turned around and headed in the direction that I had come. Gathering speed as I did, the clouds covered most of my vision of the ground on my return, but I knew I was heading in the right direction. My body had assumed a vertical position again. You couldn't make this up.

I came to a natural stop, looking down to my left I could see the hospital I have given more than half of my life to. And below, I could see the outline of my neighbourhood. I descended slowly, but I remembered the fact that I was landing in a built-up area. I quickly gained speed in my descent, and before I knew it, I was in my back garden, activating my outdoor garden light as I did. My patio door was still open. I walked inside and sat on my nursing home chair.

I'd been out of the house ten minutes, and in that time, I had been to Brighton and back. I had smelt the salty sea air and met a canine called Jimmy. I relaxed closed my eyes and thanked Metatron in my head.

"Thank you for the gifts I now have," I said. "Thank you."

Without being in a dream or being in the white room, I could hear Metatron's voice, "Do not thank me, Aaron, thank the earth."

I opened my eyes, and I was back in my dressing gown.

"Time for bed," I thought to myself. "Let's see what tomorrow brings."

NINE
Self-Healing

I woke up on the roof of my house. I nearly had a heart attack.

"How on earth did I get here?" I thought to myself, scratching my head. I was still in my dressing gown, but I was outside on top of my roof. My roof had a flat section where an attic window would have gone if I ever decided to have my loft converted into another bedroom. If the small flat surface wasn't there, I would have just rolled off. My first instinct was to get down, but I was two storeys high. The sun was just rising, and the streetlights were still lit. The breeze caught me off guard, as I only had my dressing gown on as it whipped up inside of it. I sat up and tried to think about how I'd got up here. Did I fly? Did I project myself here? Either way, I had to get down before anybody saw me. I lowered myself from the flat surface which joined onto the slope. Slowly, on my bottom, using my heels as anchors, I shuffled down the sloped part of the roof.

I was making my way towards the gutter at the edge of the house. From my roof, I could see the neighbouring homes across the street, all in darkness. Just one place lit up with pink curtains and teddy bears and dolls lining the upstairs front bedroom windowsill. It was going to be difficult, but I needed to get down and fast. If I hung from the guttering, lowering myself so that my arms and legs were dangling, my feet would only be one floor away from the ground. Trying to do this in my dressing gown, and nothing else underneath, was a task in itself.

"I can do this," I thought to myself. As I did, I pushed away from the wall. The free fall from the room appeared to happen in slow motion. I landed on both feet and let out an almighty scream of pain. Falling backwards, onto my bottom, both hands also took the impact. The pain as I hit the ground was incredible. I looked at my feet, and my right foot was facing the wrong way. No blood, no bruising, just a foot bent backwards and facing the completely wrong direction for a right foot. My dressing gown was wide open, revealing all and sundry.

Mr Williams opened his bedroom window and shouted down to me, "Are you ok Aaron?"

"Yeah," I disguised the pain in my voice. "Tripped over. I've sprained my ankle, I think."

He just stared at me. I didn't say anything else, "It looks more than a sprain to me."

"No honestly, I'm good," I said, recovering my dignity and hobbling into the house.

The nursing home chair had never looked so inviting. I eased myself into it and examined my right foot which was flopping about.

"Oh boy," I said to myself. It made me feel sick to see my foot attached to my leg but dangling around loosely. Then I remembered what Metatron had told me about healing.

Without thinking, my body began to glow. I looked at my deformed right foot. The pain I had was disappearing. I could feel it exiting my body. It was like squeezing a spot and getting the puss to the surface. Without any signs or pre-warning, my foot suddenly sprung back into the correct form. I wiggled my toes and did a rotation of my foot from left to right. At that moment, Mr Williams came running around and was banging on the back gate.

"Are you ok, Aaron? Do you need an ambulance?" He continued knocking on my back garden gate. I got up from the chair and walked around towards him. No pain, nothing. I could fully weight-bear as if nothing had happened.

I opened the gate and told Mr Williams that I was fine, he wanted to see my ankle and foot, "Let me see. Let me see!" he said persistently.

"I'm ok, honestly look," I said as I wiggled my foot around. "I must have dislocated it, but it's gone back into place now."

"Aaron, you have been fortunate," he said. "That could have been a lot worse. Are you sure you're ok, can I get you anything?"

"I'm fine honestly, but thank you," I assured him as I ushered him out from the closure of the gate and shut it behind him. "I'm going to the shops later," I shouted over the gate. "If you need anything, drop me a note."

I clicked the kettle for a hot coffee and wondered how I got on the roof of my house. I have had some wonderful experiences lately, but this one was not one of them. The coffee was refreshing and gave me the morning kick that I needed. The only explanation I could think of is that I projected myself out onto my roof during my sleep. Or that I went through the ceiling and roof. Metatron did say that I could walk through material objects.

I looked at my foot again. I just couldn't believe it. This was the best thing ever. I'd never had a broken bone before. Seeing the dangling foot, dislocated or broken, then seeing it spring back to normal, I couldn't help but smile.

"This is happening to me. This is happening to me," I repeated to myself shaking my head.

Finishing my coffee and heading upstairs, I thought again about how I ended up on the roof. I laid on my bed, looking up at the ceiling.

I relaxed my mind and took some deep breaths in and out. I concentrated on the ceiling. I thought to myself, "Right, let's do this, let's go to the ceiling."

I couldn't see the gold aura surround my body, but I could feel it. Always the same feeling. The feeling of my cells waking up. I felt the bed, beneath me, leave me. It felt as if I was falling as the bed pulled away. I was floating upwards to the ceiling, and I had to reach out with both my hands to prevent myself from hitting it.

I was on the ceiling, hands pushing away so my face didn't hit it. My toes bent resting on the surface. I closed my eyes and felt the ceiling on my fingertips. I could feel the ceiling as if it was alive. Its molecules felt like they were dancing around me, like pins and needles. My golden aura permeated the surface of the ceiling around my fingertips and extended outwards like ripples of smoke. My hands slid through the ceiling, beginning at my fingers, right up to my knuckles. I pulled both hands out fast. This was weird, weirder than flying, weirder than transporting myself to work, and even more bizarre than my foot healing on its own. It was strange to me. It felt more unnatural than any other skill I had acquired.

Slowly I placed my hands on the ceiling again, and the golden aura spread out over the surface as my hands seeped through, this time to my wrists. I let it continue up to my elbows, and then I just decided to go for it.

I closed my eyes and took a big deep breath as if I was about to dive into a cold pool. I could feel my body as it went through the ceiling. It felt like I was walking through different layers of mud. I could feel the plaster's different density, the wooden floorboards, and then the thickness of the insulation.

I opened my eyes and the golden glow was fading from out of my body. Soon I was in darkness. As my eyes adjusted, I could see daylight breaking through tiny holes in the roof where the tiles overlap each other. I was in my roof space.

At least I know how I got up here now. The golden glow was still emanating out of my body. I could make out the latch to my loft access. Lowering the ladders, I came back down the regular way. As I made my way down the ladders, it occurred to me that I could easily have floated or flown down from the rooftop earlier. Instead of dangling, falling, and breaking my foot, and then showing all of myself to Mr Williams.

I made my way back to my bed and laid on it. I remembered back to Brandon at the hospital, showing me the video of me materialising out of thin air. I hoped that he had deleted it.

Grabbing my iPhone, I went to the YouTube app. I typed in Brandon's video's title. 'appearing man'. It populated a list of videos, none from Brandon's channel. So I typed in Brandon's full name 'Brandon James', and his channel popped up. His face in the profile with two thumbs up at the camera. His latest video was four weeks old. Thankfully, he'd deleted the offending video.

I went back to the search bar on YouTube out of curiosity, and the words I had typed were still there, 'appearing man'. The top video in the search was posted ten hours ago. I clicked on it. It was a grainy webcam recording of the sea in Brighton titled, 'Brighton's Sunset Webcam' and in brackets '(unexplained appearing man)'. It had already had 21,000 views.

"Shit."

TEN
Coming Out

O pening the door to the coffee shop, the smell of coffee and sweet, decadent cakes and cookies filled my nostrils. It was a lot busier than usual. It had the lunch hour hum. There was the odd seat available dotted around. I had never seen it so busy. The sound of people chatting quietly over the ambient music, people reading, working on laptops, sitting with headphones on. A group of four well-dressed elderly ladies sat on two sofas facing each other, which is where we would typically sit.

Barkley was seated at the left of the doorway in the window facing out; sat on a high stool with three other empty seats around the table. Barkley's body pointed towards the window but he was looking at his coffee mug.

Before I joined the queue for a coffee, I tapped Barkley on the shoulder and pulled him from wherever he was in his head. "Hey Barkley," I said.

"Aaron, sorry I was miles away then. Are you ok mate?"

"Yeah good, you want another coffee?"

"Yeah, go on then cheers, just a black coffee please,"

"Great."

I took off my jacket and hung it onto the chair opposite Barkley, "Won't be long".

There were three people in the queue before me, two men and a woman. I recognised the woman but could not quite remember where from. She looked to be in her late forties, bleached blonde short spiky hair, and heavy eye makeup. The two guys that were with her carried matching large equipment bags over their shoulders. In one hand, the taller guy held a tripod, and the other smaller, balding man was holding what looked to be a boom microphone. It looked like he had a dead grey squirrel in his hand attached to a pole. I thought that they were perhaps media students about to make a film or documentary. College was only two streets away and the coffee shop was always full of students.

I looked at the woman again and gave her another smile. As I did, I realised where I had seen her before. She was a news anchor from our local TV station 'Yorkshire@'.

I couldn't quite remember her name, but I recognised her. The tall man with the tripod was at the counter and placed the order for the three of them. I was staring at the woman, and she looked back at me and smiled at me as if to say 'yes, it is me'. She had an oversized red waterproof coat on which was open, revealing a black dress underneath. It was the kind of dress that didn't fit in with the afternoon coffee shop, more of an evening meal kind of a dress.

As her eyes left me with the smile still on her face, she glanced across and made eye contact with one of the approaching older women who was making a beeline for her.

"Hi, are you Darcey Dyson from Yorkshire@?" she said.

"That's me, I'm afraid."

"Wow," she said. "You look so petite in real life."

"I get that a lot," she said in reply.

"Do you mind if I get a photo of you with my friends and me over by the sofas?" she asked.

"Of course," she said and headed over to the sofas where the other elderly women were.

The two men ahead of me carried on as if this was all part and parcel of the job.

"What brings you into Redgrand?" said one of the ladies.

I had my back to them so I could not quite make out which one said it. I listened tentatively, turning my head slightly to the right so that my right ear could pick up anything interesting.

"Nothing much happens newsworthy around here," one of the ladies continued. "Unless you're reporting on the mayor and his affair with Councillor Mullaney?"

The four women chuckled louder than was comfortable. I could feel the excitement that was buzzing around them with a local celebrity in their midst.

"No nothing that exciting," Darcey said. "I'm doing a positive piece today. You know the kind of news they slot in between the bad news, or the one that they add to the end of the bulletin to make you smile."

"Oh, how exciting!" I heard one of them say, "What time is it going to be on air? Yorkshire at 1? Yorkshire at 6? Or Yorkshire at 8?"

"Never mind what time is it going to be on," I heard another lady say. "What is the good news for our town that's worthy of making it to the TV?".

The ladies fell silent.

"You probably might have heard already, but your local theatre has won a half a million-pound grant from the arts council."

"The Civic? Has it? Oh, that's good! They might put the ticket prices down then!" They all laughed in response.

Redgrand Civic was three shops down from the coffee shop. I used to go there when I was a child to see the local pantomime at Christmas with my parents. It was a family tradition until I hit about thirteen years old, and I didn't want to go anymore. Mum and dad still went and kept up the tradition right up until their deaths.

I heard Darcey say, "It might not even make the news. I do slots like this all the time and it depends what else comes across the news desk as to whether it airs or not."

I heard the digital click of a camera and then she said, "Thank you, ladies, it was nice to meet you."

She brushed past me and grabbed one of the coffees from the counter, "Are we ready?" she said to the two guys, and off they went, the four ladies waving to her as she left.

I brought over our coffees, and Barkley looked up and gave me a smile with his big brown eyes.

"Somethings wrong isn't it?" I said. I could see the sadness in his eyes.

"Kim has walked out on me. She's gone back to her mothers. It's over this time mate."

I had been in this same situation with Barkley before, Kim must break up with him at least every three months.

"What's happened this time?" I asked, exasperated.

"We had a silly argument over what film we were going to watch last night. It was supposed to be a romantic movie night." He looked at the lid on his coffee cup. "And before you say anything, it is definitely over this time, I just know it, she just grabbed some things and walked out."

"She's done this before," I said. "Things will sort themselves out, they always do."

I was trying to reassure him. I knew they would work it out. They were the kind of couple that could not sit down and talk rationally. Hence, each heated moment always ended up in some emotional torment usually lasting a couple of days. Barkley sulks, Kim sulks, and then the next thing you know their Facebook feeds become inundated with 'love yous' and selfies of them snuggling into each other.

"No, this time it's different," he said.

"That's what you said to me last time BB, and the time before that as well. You guys need to learn how to communicate with each other is all."

He took a big drink from his coffee cup and sighed.

I wanted to tell him about my new abilities. I wanted to show him what I could do. I wanted to share my story with him so that I could have another person's perspective. Of all my friends, I would only tell Barkley because I knew it would stay with him if I did. I trusted Barkley with my life. I couldn't tell him, though, not here anyway. Although I trust him entirely, this was too big a deal to tell anyone right now. If I were to tell Barkley, it would have to be in a place of privacy. I did not want to become a rat in a science laboratory. I wasn't going to risk that.

I was about to take a drink from my cup when I heard a woman's scream from outside. It was a shriek that pierced the air, loud enough to be heard in the coffee shop through the glass window. The four elderly well-dressed women stood up and moved towards the full-length window to see what was going on.

Barkley looked out and said, "Oh my god, Aaron!"

The coffee shop hum stood still as people stopped what they were doing and looked out of the window.

Darcey Dyson was across the street. No longer wearing her red coat, she had a gun pressed against her forehead. The two men from earlier were there too. It looked as if she was filming a segment with the Civic Theatre as the backdrop.

The man holding the gun was wearing a dark blue all in one boiler suit, a black balaclava, and brown leather gloves. We could not hear what he was saying, but the look of evil and anger in his eyes was evident.

As soon as the people in the coffee shop realised what was going on outside, the atmosphere changed rapidly. People were shrieking. Panic filled the room as if an explosion had gone off. Some people were moving to the back of the room, others using their mobile phones and speaking to the emergency services. One of the old ladies started crying saying, "Do something! Someone, do something!"

Barkley shot his stool back and, without even acknowledging me, rushed past heading straight for the door.

"BB!" I shouted as he ran outside.

He ran straight into the middle of the road, the two cars that were passing stopped for Barkley. Realising the situation that was unfolding around them, they abandoned their vehicles and headed into the coffee shop.

The door was still open from when Barkley pulled at it. We could hear the gunman shouting at the two crewmen, "Stay where you are! Do not move, keep filming, I want this to be on every channel."

Barkley stood in the middle of the road. He had his back to me in the coffee shop. I could hear the adrenalin in BB's voice.

"Put the gun down," Barkley said as he took two steps nearer to Darcey and the gunman.

"Stay where you are!" the gunman shouted back at Barkley. "I only want one death today, don't make it two."

Barkley looked back at me through the window, he was in too deep, and he knew it, he gave me that look as if to say, 'Idiot I've screwed up here', but determined, he turned around and shouted the same again.

"Put the gun down," he took two more steps closer.

The blast from the gun ricocheted around the buildings and hit the coffee shop window. The shop erupted in screams with people shouting and heading for cover, turning tables over to hide behind, and people running behind the counter. The gunman had shot his gun into the air at this point. I realised that his gun was real. He said he had only wanted one death today; this man meant business.

During the panic and the screams, I ran to the toilets, I locked myself in a cubicle and took a deep breath in and slowly exhaled my controlled breath.

I could feel my cells coming alive. The orange glow that I had become accustomed to had begun. I was transforming. The golden cape and boots and the purple suit and the golden light illuminated the cubicle. I could only imagine what it would have looked like from outside the booth. If anyone were in the toilets with me, it would have looked like a fire inside this cubicle. I didn't want to walk through the shop dressed in this purple and gold suit. Behind the toilet on the wall was a small smoked glassed window, I could see daylight outside, so I knew it was an outside wall. I put my hands onto the wall on either side of the window and concentrated. The golden energy around my body intensified as my hands slowly started to submerge into the chipped white tiles. I took a breath, closed my eyes and walked forward through the wall and window. Outside, I looked up at the sky, and within microseconds, I was up in the air with a birds-eye view of the coffee shop watching the unfolding scene.

Barkley had moved closer to Darcey and the gunman. The cameraman was shaking, and the sound operator had the microphone resting on the floor. He was standing behind the cameraman.

Darcey was pale white with shock. The silent tears of fear falling from her eyes mixed with black mascara and eye shadow. They ran down both sides of her face making her look even paler. Not moving, she was frozen with fear.

The gunman grabbed Darcy's hand and spun her around, pulling the back of her head onto his chest. With his left arm, he wrapped it across her neck, and she screamed as he flung her around like a rag doll.

Darcey was now facing Barkley. The gunman took the gun from the side of Darcey's head and pointed it directly at Barkley, "Stay back, or I will shoot!" He flipped the weapon back and forth from Darcey's head to Barkley and back.

I was still up in the air looking down at the situation. I was aware that people could see me; I didn't care. I had to make sure no one got hurt. I could see flashes of light from the upstairs windows of the shops.

I was being photographed. At this point, I did not have one fleeting worry about being seen. I had to immobilise this idiot with the gun before he hurt or killed someone. Considering the situation, I was in, I felt calm and collected.

"Put down the gun and release the woman," I said.

My voice sounded powerful and dominant. If I hadn't been in the situation I was in, I would have made a joke of myself.

The gunman and Darcey looked up. Darcey's face changed from fearful and tense, to shock and bewilderment. The cameraman swung his camera around and up, pointing it at me in the sky. This was it, from that moment, I realised there was no going back.

The gunman took a step back in shock and dragged Darcey backwards with him. "What the... Who the..."

He pointed the gun up into the air and directed it at me. His hand was shaking so much the gun looked like it was vibrating.

The gunman in shock stuttered, "What is this? Some kind of stunt?"

Darcey looked at his shaking hand saw an opportunity, she attempted to knock the gun out of his hand.

The gun went off, and Barkley fell to the floor.

Screams and panic came from all around. Barkley lay on the floor, bleeding out.

The gunman still had the gun in his hand and, pushing it into the side of Darcey's head, shouted at Darcey, "I said I only wanted one death today!"

I looked at the gun he was holding. Concentrating, I imagined being part of the gun. I could feel the molecules the weapon was made up of, I'd made a connection with it. The gold aura surrounding my body was now around the gun too. I had locked in with it. There were no more bullets coming from this gun.

I imagined the gun being in my hand. The gun looked to have an invisible force, as if it was being pulled out of the gunman's hand by someone invisible. That someone was me. I wasn't physically grabbing it, my mind was. His grip was getting tighter, trying to hold onto it. Eventually, he let go, and the gun floated over to me. I heard the crowd gasp in amazement. I grabbed hold of the gun, and our golden auras became one. I floated down, landed on the ground, and ran towards Barkley.

"Hey, hey," I said. "Barkley open your eyes."

He slowly opened his eyes. "Hi," he said. He looked at me and checked out the golden aura surrounding me, "Am I dead?" he said.

"No," I replied and smiled at him. "What were you thinking?" I asked.

"It was a gut reaction, I don't know. Is that woman ok?" He tried to look over, but the pain held him back as he grimaced and realised he was injured.

"She's fine," I said. "Let me look at you. You're bleeding badly."

He had taken the bullet in the left side of his chest just below the left clavicle, "Any closer to the right and it would have been your heart," I said.

"Hold still," I said as I placed my hand on his wound. By now, a small crowd was gathering. The gunman had gone. The cameras were still rolling, and flashes of lights were coming from phones all around us. The eerie silence around us did not match the scene that we had just witnessed. The silence of bewilderment filled the air.

"What are you doing?" he said.

"Keep still, it won't take long."

I connected with Barkley, and I could feel his life source, his soul. His eyes locked with mine, and he looked at me as if he knew it was me. He looked back over his shoulder to see where we were sitting in the coffee shop window. I know he was looking for me.

I could feel the damage in his body in the form of energy. The dark smoky circles of energy that were hurting him, causing him to bleed out, came to the surface of his chest wall and entered my hand. Slowly, out came a bullet, which popped up out of his skin, and then his shirt, and rolled off his shoulder onto the floor with a ting noise as the metal hit the concrete. There was a small hole in his shirt where the bullet had pierced it, and underneath you could see an open wound. The golden energy stretched from my hand to his shoulder like lightning in slow motion, I could see the wound close.

"Healed," I said.

"Healed?" he said, pulling his shirt back to reveal perfect skin, crusted with blood. "How?" he looked at me and stared straight into my soul. "What?"

Barkley could not catch his words. He was dumbfounded and, for the first time in a long time, speechless. I smiled at him and stood up.

The crowd that had gathered took a step back in fear and uncertainty.

Darcey Dyson came running over. The cameraman followed her, now with the camera on his shoulder. She held a microphone in her hand and thrust it into my face.

"How did you.... Where did you?... What do we call you?"

I didn't know what to say; my reaction was impassive.

I didn't have a name! I was calling myself Purple Man! I was just about to say, 'Purple Man', when I remembered Caroline from the hospital. How excited and alive she looked when she saw my golden aura.

"My name is iLUMiNO," I said, and I looked up to the sky and flew upwards.

The crowd gathered around Darcey and the cameraman as she addressed what had just happened to the camera.

She didn't even care that two minutes ago she had a gun in her face. Darcey was a reporter, and she had the most significant news scoop in the history of humanity. Barkley got up from the ground and headed to the coffee shop. I landed at the back of the shop, placing my hands on the outside wall, resonating myself onto the frequency, I walked through it.

Once inside the toilet cubicle, I closed my eyes and powered down. The golden aura faded, and I was Aaron Abbey again. Quickly I rushed back to the shop and hung around with the other people who were still cowering under tables.

"Aaron, Aaron!" Barkley shouted as he rushed into the shop front.

"Over here," I said, getting up from one of the tables. I rushed over and could see the blood on Barkley's shirt, "You're hurt!" I said. "Are you ok? Is that your blood?"

He pulled his shirt back to reveal his healed skin, "I'm ok."

"You stupid man!" I said. "What were you thinking?"

He took a step back and looked at me closely.

"That's exactly what he said to me."

ELEVEN
Sniper On The Roof

Leigh and Adam's housewarming party was in full swing. Guests were still arriving, and Leigh and Adam were the perfect hosts. Topping people's drinks up, showing them around the apartment, and directing them to a table full of prepared party food. I was out on the terrace overlooking the night sky with a can of beer in my hand. I was undecided if I was going to attend, but I chose to get ready and go at the last minute. I wanted to spend some time with my friends. It had been seven days since iLUMiNO had made an appearance and it was all the world was talking about.

Theories had filled the internet all over the world. Everyone had an opinion of what happened. Countless eyewitnesses uploading photos and videos, making money, and selling them to news channels. It was the talk of work; it was the talk of the town, it was the talk of the world. Everywhere I went, people were talking about it. Every TV channel was reporting on the same subject. *Who was he? Where did he come from? Was he an alien from outer space?*

Religious leaders, politicians, sci-fi writers, famous actors, people who worked on special effects in film studios, these people were all taking the seat on various news channels, and guest shows, just to talk about me.

Conspiracy theories were making me sound like some sort of alien. Some were saying I was the messiah, or the second coming, some people focused on debunking it and putting evidence together to disprove me, which even made for good watching. All of my close friends had rung me, or texted me, 'Have you seen the news?' 'You were there; are you ok?' But I heard nothing from Barkley. Nothing.

Barkley had become a local celebrity in his own right. After the event, he was taken straight to the hospital and checked over. Darcey Dyson and the news crew went with him and conducted a full interview with him in his A&E cubicle.

Darcey Dyson was in the studio within two hours of Barkley's interview. She was no longer on the streets doing outside interviews. Now she was at the news desk; full hair and makeup, next to the regular news presenter.

It was breaking news. News channels repeating the story over and over again. It dominated the news for twenty four hours. There had been reports of internet outages in some areas of the world. YouTube channels crashing with people trying to see the so-called iLUMiNO.

The gunman had been arrested and caught soon after. He was wrestled to the ground down a back alley trying to take off his boiler suit; revealing a suit and tie and crisp white shirt. If he'd have walked out wearing that, no-one would have suspected it was him. It turns out it was Darcey Dyson's husband who wanted her dead for cheating on him. Her marriage was over, but her career was just starting.

The world had changed. It was a feeding frenzy for the media, but so many questions remained unanswered. I looked at all the pictures and photographs and listened with interest to what people were saying about me, but I didn't see myself. I didn't feel pressured, victimised, or anything about the photos or discussions of iLUMiNO. I know it was me, but it didn't feel like me. I had, or felt like I had, an emotional detachment which was probably a good thing. Our local town had become a media circus. People from all over the world were coming to the street to see where it happened in the hopes of seeing this enigma, hoping that he would turn up again. News cameras and reporters filled the street and had done so for days. News vans with huge satellite dishes filled the streets. The coffee shop had never been so busy.

Leigh and Adam headed over to me, still on the balcony, holding hands.

"Hey Az," Leigh said. "You ok, pal? I've put some food together, please have some. I'd hate it to go to waste."

"Sure, I'll have a bite later."

"Everything ok?" she said.

Adam didn't even give me a chance to reply, "I heard you were at the shooting the other day. Must have been awful. And Barkley, poor man," he said shaking his head then taking a drink from an oversized gin glass filled with fruits.

"I'm fine, honestly. I couldn't see much from where I was in the coffee shop, but yeah the entire experience has been somewhat sensationalised."

"What's your take on this Iloomus guy?" He said, taking another big drink from the glass.

"iLUMiNO," I corrected him.

"Yeah, whatever! Oh, excuse me," he said "look who it is," as he saw one of his theatre friends walking in with a big bunch of flowers. Leigh recognised her straight away and stayed put next to me. "Oh, here she is. Beulah big bust, swanning in, taking over with her look at me look at my cleavage face". Leigh finished bitching and turned around to look out over the balcony. I turned out towards the balcony with her and drank some beer from my can.

"She's ok. I just can't stand her," she said, then took a drink of her neat vodka. There was a silence that befell us both as we just stared into the night sky of Redgrand. The sky was cloudy, but when it did break the moonlight was beautiful.

"So come on, spit," she said, turning around to face me with her hand on her hip. "I know you, and something is going on in that head of yours." She prodded my head and smiled at me. "Come on, spit it out, tell your Auntie Leigh."

"It's nothing, there is nothing, honestly. I'm fine."

"Well," she said, taking a drink of her vodka, "Tell your face!" she laughed. "So long as you are ok, Pal. I don't want my Aaron going funny on me, that's my job."

She turned around, and Adam and Beulah stood in front of us, Beulah produced a massive bunch of flowers and presented them to Leigh.

"Here you are my darling; I just couldn't turn up empty-handed. These might brighten up your new place. Which, by the way, is beautiful."

Leigh snatched them from her hand. "Thank you," she said, walking past her. Leigh turned around and mouthed to me, "I don't even own a vase."

"Beulah, this is Aaron," Adam said, introducing me. I already knew of this lady; I had seen her many times in various stage productions. She was an amateur actress, and I had seen her in several shows throughout the years. She could command an audience as soon as she entered a room. Dressed in a long slim black and gold leopard print dress with sewn-in gold glitter that sparkled as she walked across the room, she was a sight to behold. The dress had a slit at the front hip that showed just enough leg to keep her dignity and a low cut neckline that didn't leave much to the imagination. Her leopard print hat was massive, it was the one you would wear at a race night, or a wedding, certainly not to an indoor housewarming party. But this woman carried it; she was a class act. I do not know how she took care of any personal hygiene because her nails were so long. She was in her mid-forties, and you could tell she worked hard on her appearance. You could tell that she took care of everything from her skin to her muscle tone and body shape. Her hair was long, dark brown nearly black, she had it swept to one side in a chignon, and it hung from her left shoulder onto her chest.

She twiddled with her hair as she was talking to me. This woman meant business. Everyone knew her, and nearly everyone warmed to her, clearly not Leigh.

"Be a darling?" she said, "and grab me a champagne."

Leigh and Adam had a small table draped in a white cloth with three champagne bottles and glasses for guests to have as they came in.

I poured the champagne into two glasses, and Leigh floated past me as I did.

"She's not even brought anything to drink. She will be as thirsty as those flowers she brought me".

"Don't be ungrateful," I said, "they are lovely flowers."

"Oh, I'm not!" she said. "I've just not got anywhere to put them. They look lovely in my bathtub!"

We both laughed. I brought the drink over to Beulah. We talked about shows she had appeared in. Telling me funny stories, backstage antics, or things going wrong, it was a nice break and pleasant distraction from people talking about iLUMiNO all the time.

She told me how she was now over the fact that she was never making it big as an actress. How fortunate she was to have a husband who could support her financially. She was grateful for the cards that life had dealt her. She was able to follow her dream, even though it was mainly amateur productions, she was appreciative.

"How do you do it?" I asked.

"What's that, dear?"

"How do you learn all those lines and remember where to be at certain times? The moves? How do you become that character?"

"Blocking, dear. It's called blocking. In rehearsal, we block a move to a direct or indirect narrative, or a thought process, the character may be having.

Lines come very easily to me, my dear. I am lucky enough to have a photographic memory. The rehearsal process is when you begin to breathe life into a character. You step in and out of that character intermittently during rehearsals. The director gives you new drections, new suggestions all the time. It's not until towards the end of the process, all of the intricacies come together that you begin to feel the person you are portraying."

"Do you feel like you are one hundred percent the character?" I questioned her.

"No, love. I don't," she said. "Maybe ninety percent of me does, but I am still me. There is always a part of me concentrating on what comes next; what line, or action, or sound effect. If I were to become the character fully, then there wouldn't be a play. The character would probably think what the hell am I doing on a stage! You might read interviews of actors telling you they completely took on the role of the character. Nonsense, there has to remain an element of self. Otherwise, you would lose your mind."

I thought for a moment about what she was telling me. She was describing how I felt as iLUMiNO. I was myself, but at the same time, I felt like I was another person or character. She didn't realise, but she helped me understand how I could fit into this world as iLUMiNO.

I felt like I was sucking all the knowledge from her. I wanted more from her. Beulah loved the fact that someone was interested in her passion; her craft. Listening to her intently. I realised I had an empty champagne glass, and Beulah's was still full.

"Help yourself to another drink, my love. I'll go and circulate a bit. Lovely to chat to you Aaron," and off she swooned to the outside patio table. In the corner of the decking, all four of the guests stood up and cheered, "Hello Beulah!" and put their arms out to embrace her.

I glanced at my phone for the time and then looked across to the apartment's front door, Barkley was a no show. I was disappointed. He was probably in a studio somewhere in London doing another interview. I looked at my messages that I'd sent him over the last week, each one said 'read' underneath, but not one reply. I assumed he was too busy with his whirlwind of fame. Either that, or I had seriously upset him. "Maybe it's because I didn't rush out with him to save the reporter woman," I thought to myself. "I'm not like that though," having an internal discussion with myself. Barkley always finds himself in difficult circumstances. It's in his DNA to rush into a situation without thinking it through first. That was his nature. I hoped he was ok wherever he was. I sent another text message.

'Hope you're ok buddy; you've gone quiet on me, give me a shout when you get this'.

Underneath the message, the word 'sent' changed to 'read'.

Sliding my phone back into my pocket, Penelope waved at me through the glass sliding doors. She was stting on the settee with a miniature poodle sat on her lap waving me over. Penelope was known as the 'lady in pink'. It was all she wore, it was her favourite colour. In high school, all her accessories would be pink, her coat, bag, ribbons in her hair, even her stationary would be pink. The pink bombshell that she has become was now her trademark; she would not be the same if she turned up wearing any other colour but pink. Her little apricot dog sat on her lap so obedient just looking out at the people before it. Penelope Kidder had the most beautiful eyes you ever would see. Big and beautiful. If you did not know Penelope and you saw a photograph of her, you would assume she had used a filter to make her eyes more prominent. They were naturally big; she would accentuate them with white eyeliner. However, she didn't need to do this; her eyes were probably still as beautiful without makeup.

Pen was a writer; she had always been a good storyteller. I loved the fact that I was a friend of an author. She had published a series of children's books and was in the middle of making a deal with a television company to serialise it for children's television. 'The Faery Tales of Rosie Quartz'. It was all she ever talked about, but we loved her for it. I was as proud as she was. I'd never read her books, but I supported her all the way. I was in awe of her creativeness. I only ever got to see Pen if we had gatherings like this, friends' birthdays, weddings, garden parties and whatnot. It was the same with Brenda, who was sat quietly beside Pen. Brenda was another friend of mine from high school. She was the boffin of our high school group, and it showed, as she was now teaching. She was the quietest amongst us, very rarely had anything to add to a conversation, she was a good listener and infrequently gave her opinion. She would keep things close to her chest, but occasionally when Brenda did have an opinion, it was always right, even if she was wrong. Just because she was small, petite, and still looked like she did when we were at school, did not mean that she couldn't stand up for herself, or on her own two feet. If she had something to say, she would say it and boy would we know about it when Brenda opened her mouth. I liked to catch up with my old buddies from school.

I made my way over, and they both stood up and gave me a group hug.

"Hi, Aaron, how are you doing?" Penelope said.

"Hi Aaron," Brenda said, pulling me in tight, and cuddling me. "We were just talking about the iLUMiNO man. You were there weren't you, with Barkley? Is it true what they showed us on TV? Did he really fly in from the sky and make the gun float in mid-air? And Barkley, did he save him from the bullet?"

Penelope added, "It sounds too farfetched to be believable, but it's what they're reporting."

"So, come on, spill," Brenda continued. "We want it first hand, what happened?"

They both leaned in as if they were about to get some juicy gossip and listened intently.

"Honestly, I didn't see anything. I was at the back of the coffee shop the whole time. I remember seeing the gun in Darcey's forehead. Barkley ran out; then all hell broke loose in the coffee shop. When he fired the bullet in the air, we all ran to the back of the shop and hid behind tables. I missed all the real fun. I didn't know anything about this iLUMiNO guy until Barkley came back into the shop and told me."

They both sat back as if disappointed with the answer.

"You mean you were witness to the most remarkable thing on earth that's ever happened, and you hid behind a table?"

"Pen," I said, "It wasn't like that. People were screaming, they were scared. I was scared. We didn't know what was to unfold next!" They both sat in silence; disappointed that I couldn't update them or confirm the news footage was real.

Brenda said," Barkley will know, he might be coming, we'll ask him if he gets here."

"Good luck with that," I said. "I think the fame has gone to his head."

"Sniff of jealousy, Brenda? Can you smell it?" Penelope said.

They both sniffed into the air and laughed, just as Lottie came and sat on the opposite armchair.

"I can't stay long," she said. "I've got to get back to the twins. They are at that funny age when they don't want me to go out in case I get shot or taken away by an alien. Goddamn news, it messes with children's heads, there is no getting away from it. Especially with this fake buffoon trying to be something he's not. As if the world hasn't got enough to cope with! Anyway, are you all right? It's nice to see you all." She looked around as if looking for something, "Has she put some food on? I'm starving."

Leigh was walking past and happened to hear Lottie talking about her take on the fake iLUMiNO. She perched on the back of the chair and joined in on the conversation. "There's a table of food at the back Lottie, go and fill your boots love."

The room was full of people I knew of but didn't know well enough to talk to. Beulah was still doing the rounds like a butterfly flitting in and around people. Adam was with a group of lads I didn't know, but our little corner of the room was filling up with my close friends. It was comforting, the atmosphere was pleasant. I felt homely and safe. I only needed Barkley here, and it would have been the same people who were with me at my 21st birthday party. The day my life changed forever.

"So, you think it's all a fraud then, faked?" Leigh said.

"Oh yeah! Are you kidding me - course it is. Come on, you guys don't believe this, do you?" Lottie replied.

Brenda, Penelope and Leigh didn't answer we just looked at her.

"Oh, guys come on, it's a fake. One big fat fake. Look at Darcey or whatever she calls herself. She's now on all mainstream media channels. She's a 'made' woman now. She will be doing a book next week. Ok..." she leant in and got more comfortable. "Think about it, there just happened to be a cameraman and a sound man and a reporter on the scene. It was her husband who had the gun, who just happens to be an actor, the perfect person to plan a story like this. As for Barkley... Hey, where is Barkley?" she said, looking around for him. "Well," She continued, "He was just in the wrong place at the wrong time. The gunman fired a blank at him with special effect blood, which was meant for Darcey."

Lottie looked at us all with conviction in what she was saying, awaiting a reply. We all sat in silence. "Come on! Please tell me you don't believe in a man floating down and having superhuman powers, do you?"

Leigh cleared her throat and said, "Well, I know what you're saying, and I guess to some extent I am kind of on your bus. But, oh I don't know, it just looked so real on TV. I've seen this YouTube channel saying what you just said, and they have analysed the footage, and they said you could see a wire, and a blurred out crane in the background. But I'll be honest, I'm on the fence."

Penelope said, "Well I believe it to be true. I was so hoping Aaron would have been able to give me more of an insight, but 'chicken shit Aaron' saw the back of a table instead."

"Hey, less of the shit," Leigh said, rolling her eyes at me.

"Sorry Aaron, I was just hoping for some good home-grown facts. I guess I've not made my mind up yet until I get more info from Barkley.

I've seen him on the news, but you know what the news is like, they push a story into a narrative that they want us mere folks to believe. It's mainly always biased anyway."

"What do you think Brenda?" Lottie said as she dipped her hand into a bowl of crisps on the coffee table and shoved them in her mouth without any decorum whatsoever.

All heads turned to Brenda, knowing whatever she said we would agree with her.

"Well, if you ask me, which you are, there is a lot more to it. For a start, if he was real, well, where is he now? A one-off appearance does not qualify for anything to be real in my eyes. Darcey is making money and has already been promoted to news desk presenter, so she had an incentive. Then there is her husband, the supposed gunman, how do we know he was arrested? How do we know that he was the gunman? You read about this fake news all the time. My opinion is this..." she paused briefly. "I need more proof before I make my mind up. There you have it."

Lottie responded, "Well Barkley would have been the one to get more answers, he could have given us his account."

We all agreed.

"But where is he?" Leigh asked, "He did RSVP to me, but this was before all this had kicked off."

"Well, I've sent him text messages all week, but he's not answered one of them," I answered.

"That's not like Barkley," Leigh said. "Have you tried ringing his Kim?"

"I've not got her number," I replied. "But they did split up last week before all this happened. He was having one of his 'woe is me' moments."

"Oh hell," Leigh said. "Those two are on and off like I don't know what, but I guess it's not love if it doesn't hurt." She sighed and looked over at Adam.

"Are you two ok?" Penelope asked Leigh.

"Yeah we're great. Honestly, we're better than ever. Moving in together is just what we needed."

There was a commotion coming from the front door, cheers and whoops; we couldn't quite see around the corner. Beulah floated across the room and made her way towards the front door.

"Whoever it is, I'll let them survive 'Beulah Big Breasts' first," Leigh said as she left us, walked over to Adam, and hung from his arms, landing her head on his shoulder.

"She's pregnant," Penelope said.

"She's not. I would know," I said. "We tell each other everything."

"She's drinking water," Penelope said, taking a sip from Leigh's glass that she left on the table.

"No way."

Lottie looking around, "Well I'm not being funny but I wouldn't want to be bringing my children up in a skyrise apartment. No way!"

We all looked at her.

"What? I'm just saying!" Lottie rolled her eyes.

The buzz at the entrance had died down, and Beulah came back heading towards the champagne table. Leigh saw her heading that way and grabbed the last two glasses before Beulah could get them. Leigh held her head up high and said, "Thank you," before walking towards the front door.

I heard Leigh's electrifying laugh and then a scream of excitement from behind the corner. It made me smile. Lottie, Brenda and Pen were all chatting away, all the while Penelope was stroking her little dog and she she saw me looking at it.

"Is it a she?" I asked. "It's a miniature poodle, right?"

"Yeah she is, and she's so intelligent."

"Unlike some people we know!" Leigh quipped as she rejoined us, staring over at Beulah.

"She's called Sindee. Go ahead pat her, she loves to be the centre of attention," Penelope said with passion.

I patted the dog on her head, her tail started to wag, and she looked at me. I could have sworn I could see her smile.

"See, she likes you," Penelope remarked.

"Well surprise guys, Kim and Barkley are here," Leigh said. "He's just popping by to congratulate us. They can't stay long, but he wants to speak to you, Aaron."

Kim came around the corner and said hi to everyone in our group, followed closely by Barkley. Both with a champagne flute in their hands.

"Hey guys," Penelope said to both of them. Then she directed her next greeting to Barkley, "Hey movie star, can I have your autograph?"

The girls started laughing as Kim sat on the sofa with Penelope and Brenda, "Girls, it's been a right whirlwind." They all gathered in closer and eagerly waited for the latest gossip.

"Mate I need a word," Barkley said to me looking serious and placing his drink down on the table with no intention of drinking it. He didn't look well. He looked worn and tired, with dark circles under his eyes.

"The pressure of fame getting to you?" I said. "You haven't even replied to my texts."

"Mate, I've not replied to anybody's texts, especially not yours. Something is going on, and I need to speak to you and quickly."

He took out his mobile, left it on the coffee table next to his full flute of champagne, and walked to the outside terrace beckoning with his head for me to follow him. Leigh and Lottie have cottoned on to what is happening, partially leaving Kim's conversation, watching me head out, and only then joining back to the discussion.

"What's up, mate? You're acting strange. Are you ok?"

Barkley put his hand on his chin and says, "Look behind me."

I looked over his shoulder. I could see the streetlights and Red-grand hospital in the distance. "What? What am I looking at?"

"Top of the office block on your right mate, look!"

He was now making me feel paranoid even though I had no reason to, "Mate, I don't know what I'm looking at, the offices are in darkness."

"The roof - look at the rooftop."

My face changed, and he realised I saw what he was referring to.

On the top of the office block, next to the old style chimney blocks, was a marksman or a sniper, dressed in black. He looked to be military but I wasn't sure. He was partially in the shadows. Gun mounted on a tripod.

"There are more of them," he said. "Mate, my life's screwed."

"What do you mean?" I panicked, my voice cracking. "What's this all about? Should we be worried?"

"I don't know, I think they are waiting to see if that 'thing' comes back. Let's just say this..." he looks around tentatively. "I've been de-tained for nearly three days mate; my first interview with Darcey at the hospital was my real account; it was a real interview, I was telling the truth. I won't lie to you, Aaron." He took a deep breath and another. Then looked around to make sure no one was listening, "Since that in-terview, this team of people came in from the government and we had to sign this disclosure."

"We? Who's we?" I said.

"Me and Darcey," he continued, shifting from one foot to the next nervously. "I don't even know what I signed Aaron. The pressure was on, and since that interview, the rest have been partially scripted. I had to follow a goddam script, and I couldn't stray from it."

"The same with Darcey. I saw them put her into a car at the same time as me. They have let us go now obviously."

"Let you go?" I couldn't wrap my head around what I was hearing.

"Me and Darcey, we have been locked up for three days man. Inter-rogation, lie detectors, radiation tests."

"Radiation?"

"They've tested us both as we were the closest to the being."

It had never occurred to me, that becoming iLUMiNO could have any adverse effects on anyone's physical health. "Oh my god, and were you radioactive?"

"Well, they have released us, so I don't think we are radioactive. They've taken DNA samples from us. They've swabbed my shoulder. I've had injections, MRI scans, chest x-rays. You name it, I'm sure I've undergone every test ever created."

"This blacked-out car dropped me off in town, and my phone rang. It was an unknown number. I answered it. It was Darcey, she told me to meet her at the Saver Supermarket and hung up. I hung around the supermarket for ages, and when I finally did see her, she ignored me. As she brushed past me, she slapped this in my hand as she walked past."

Barkley slid out a cheap plastic mobile phone and a piece of paper. "There are only two people that have this number, that's Darcey and now you. I trust you mate." He dropped the piece of paper as he slid the phone back into his pocket, knowing I could see the piece of paper he said, "Don't pick it up now, wait till I've gone. Darcey said they might have our phones tapped. They are watching us, but I've nothing else to tell them."

"BB," I said, feeling guilty for what he had been put through. "You look terrible. I don't know what to say, let me fix you some food from the buffet table."

He set off towards the table, and I picked up the piece of paper with the phone number on and held it tight in my hands. I looked over at the girls with Kim sat on the sofas, "I see you and Kim are back together again," I said when I caught him up.

"Oh, yeah mate, she's all over me now that I'm goddam famous." Barkley rolled his eyes and grabbed a pastry from the table and shoved it in like it was a lettuce leaf. Chewing away with pastry flakes coming out of his mouth as he spoke, he said, "There is one more thing,"

Barkley looked at me and got closer. "That thing, that iLUMiNO, whatever it was, he knew my name." He stopped chewing and grabbed my hand and put it on his chest where the bullet had hit, closing his eyes he said, "Aaron, if I'd had been blind I would have sworn 'he' was you."

"What?" I said, pulling my hand away with a nervous laugh.

He continued "All of my senses apart from my eyes were telling me it was you that was in front of me, healing me. I just knew it. I can't explain it." He shook his head in disbelief to himself, "I mean it's absurd. Right? Just saying it out loud is weird enough."

After a brief pause, Barkley continued speaking, quieter than before, "A man flying down from out of the sky, who then levitates a gun in mid-air using some sort of telekinesis. And then, if that wasn't enough, he pulls a bullet out from my shoulder. To top it off, he then heals an open wound. It's mad, but for me to think that it was you? Hah, pal, I must be losing it!"

Neither of us spoke, I'm not very good at breaking an awkward silence.

"I wish I had seen what you had seen," I said. "It's all very traumatic. Is this what you told the military or the government people, that you thought the iLUMiNO guy was me?"

"You would think I was in the middle of a science fiction book, right? With what's happened to me over the last few days. I would say that I was the main character. No mate, I never mentioned the part about you though. Hell, I didn't even tell them that the being knew my name."

Barkley shakes his head in disbelief and looks away as if going over the scene in his head. He locked his eyes back into mine. "Aaron, he called me by my name. He said to me, 'Barkley, what the hell were you thinking?' I ran back into the coffee shop to find you and guess what? You said the precise same words to me." Barkley paused a little and looked deep into my eyes; I could tell he was trying to work out what I was thinking.

"How could he know my name, Aaron?"

I shook my head, I had the answer, but I couldn't share it with him, not here, and not right now.

He took another bite of the pasty, "Mate, my head is done in, it really is."

Barkley's cheap mobile phone began to ring from the inside of his jacket pocket. He turned his back to the gunmen on the roof as he slid it out so that he could see the screen. I could just make out a number on the green backlit LCD screen. He pressed a button which silenced the call, but you could see that it was still ringing. He slid it back into his pocket, green LCD screen flashing.

"Darcey Dyson is the only one who has this number. And you, of course. I'll go and ring her somewhere private."

He grabbed a can from my four-pack of beers which I had put on the food table as I arrived and he headed towards the toilet. Leigh pointed him in the direction of the bathroom, and off he went.

I walked back over to the railing and discretely tried to look for the sniper on the rooftop offices opposite, but I could not see anyone. Looking down to the ground, I could tell we were about thirty floors up. An empty car park lit up, a grassed area to the side with a few trees and benches that looked quiet and still, nothing out of the ordinary.

I saw headlights turn on from a black car. They shone out, lighting up one of the empty benches then the engine started. I could hear the screech of tyres trying to gain traction as it set off.

Leigh and Lottie came up behind me and linked my arms one at each side. All three of us looking out into the great beyond known as Redgrand.

Neither one of them looked at me or made eye contact with me. For half a minute, maybe longer, all three of us looked out towards the night sky and the twinkling lights of Redgrand.

Leigh broke the silence, "Something's not right."

Lottie didn't react; neither did I. A minute went past, and no one said anything. You could hear the ambient music and guests' general chit chat with the occasional outburst of laughter in the background, but we remained silent.

Lottie, realising that I didn't answer Leigh, unlinked her arm from mine and said, "I'll head back to Brenda and Penelope if you guys need to speak."

"Look, I don't care what's going off, but I know something is... Barkley came in and made a beeline for you. He looks like death warmed up, and, I don't know, but I do know something is, not right." Her hand found its way to mine, we interlocked fingers, and she rested her head on my shoulder. "I am here for you. You know that, right?" She said in a whisper filled with love.

"I know," I said, and I squeezed her hand to reinforce my answer.

"So, you would tell me wouldn't you if there was something?" She paused to find the right words... "Something wrong, or something that you needed to share? A problem halved is a..." She gave a silent pause as she realised she'd got the saying wrong... "Is a problem halved?"

I didn't answer her. I just squeezed her hand again to reassure her I was listening. She squeezed my hand back as we both continued to look out into the lights of the darkness that befell Redgrand.

"Ok," she said. "Right, I know we usually tell each other everything, we have this no holds barred friendship, my crap is your crap and vice versa blah blah blah." She paused again as if to think this through. "If there's something wrong, Aaron, if there's something you want to tell me, but you can't tell me, just squeeze my hand again."

I squeezed her hand without even thinking. I regretted it instantly. Leigh knows me inside out, as does Barkley. I just wanted to tell them what was happening, especially my friends who were with me when I found out about Mum and Dad's accident. These friends were here tonight, but tonight it wasn't about me. This was Leigh and Adam's occasion.

Leigh held onto my hand; she didn't let go.

"I knew," she said in a high-pitched voice. We continued to hold hands, and it felt like I could feel the cogs in her brain going over and over.

There was the sound of a glass smashing in the background, and neither of us looked or acknowledged it.

"Pal, I'm here for you, no matter what. You know that, don't you?"

My eyes were filling up. I loved this woman; she was able to understand me on a level no other person could.

I just squeezed her hand. I didn't want her to see I was crying.

There was a commotion in the living room; Penelope, Lottie, and Brenda grabbed Barkley and threw him on the sofa. Kim was chatting to Adam, unaware that vultures had set feast upon her Barkley.

"So, if you can't tell me what the situation is, please just tell me you're ok? You're ok, aren't you?"

We both continued to look out, neither one of us making eye contact.

I didn't answer.

She shook my hand vigorously and under her breath but in a more resonant voice; "Aaron, tell me you're ok."

I squeezed her hand slowly.

We both turned inwards to face each other, and the pair of us had tears in our eyes, she pulled me towards her and hugged the life out of me.

"Friends, for life, Pal. Friends for life," she said.

TWELVE
Live On Morning TV

Barkley had left the party soon after and he hadn't come back to speak to me. However, he did acknowledge me, giving me a wink through the double glass patio doors as he left. He gave Leigh a quick kiss on the cheek, and Adam a handshake. before whispering into Kim's ear as they left. He didn't fill me in on the phone conversation with Darcey Dyson; he went pretty much straight away.

That was two days ago.

Watching Barkley 'live' on This Morning's daytime television show being interviewed by Philip Schofield and Holly Willoughby, I listened with particular detail and interest. I wasn't shocked to see Barkley on the television. His face had filled my news feed, and my television set, since this all began.

I remembered that Barkley had told me about the 'secret government people' or whoever they were, and that they had told him to follow a script of some sort. I wanted to hear what details he had changed. I was there at the time, I know what happened, and I wanted to see how much of his detail varied from the truth.

In short, he did explain what had happened. He did not deviate from that, but he did add elements that weren't his own words. He stated that he could not be sure if it was a complete fake, like an elaborate magician's stunt. He used words like 'it appeared like" or 'it looked like' when being interviewed. Philip asked about being hit by a bullet. He said, "It's been suggested that it could have been a red paintball. Whatever it was that shot at me, the force did knock me to the ground. But again, this could still have been part of a highly sophisticated prank." He looked off-camera nervously, and the camera cut back to the presenters.

Holly interjected, "Surely, you would have known if your shoulder had a bullet in it. If your shoulder was bleeding. I am sure you would be able to tell the difference between your own blood and red paint from a paintball gun?"

Barkley had an earpiece in, I could see it, and I could see him starting to sweat under stress. He nervously looked off-camera again. He was becoming agitated. He held his left hand to his left ear as if listening to someone. He then disguised it as an itch.

"I was in shock, I guess. My adrenalin kicked in," he said. "Imagine yourself in my shoes. I initially saw a man with a gun pointed to Darcey Dyson, the woman from our regional news. Well to be honest, I was in fight or flight mode. The gun, to my knowledge at that time was real, and then when it went off, and I fell to the ground, with pain in my shoulder..." he paused. "Look, I can only tell you what I saw and what I experienced, and to me, the experience felt real, as real as I am here on the couch with you two. Look at it like this, those windows behind you, they're not letting in natural light, are they? And that isn't the river Thames or a London skyline behind you, is it? It's a video on giant screens made to look like windows with pre-recorded footage of the river Thames, so for the viewers at home, it seems like we are in a building with the River Thames behind us.

"It looks and feels as real to me as it does to the viewers at home, but because I saw it earlier, before we went live on air, I saw them as static screens. If I hadn't seen the blank screens before we went on air, then I would have thought they were real windows. That is how my experience with this iLUMiNO guy was. It felt authentic. It felt very very real. But at the same time, it could quite as easily have been an immense illusion like the ones that Dynamo does."

He paused to think and then carried on, "Was it real? I don't know. Did it feel natural and authentic to me?" He looks off camera again, then makes direct eye contact with the camera again, "Yes, it felt real to me. And if you are out there iLUMiNO, if you are watching this, come forward, show the world that you are real."

The female presenter quickly looked up from her cue cards and interrupted Barkley, "If this being, this so-called iLUMiNO was real. Barkley what would you say to him? What would you say to him right now?"

The camera slowly panned in on Barkley you could see that he was shaking, noticeable beads of sweat were gathering on his temples. He had his hands clasped fingers interlocked and was looking down towards his hands. He slowly lifted his head to the camera and said directly eyes locked as if he was only speaking to me.

"I've just said it, prove the doubters wrong iLUMiNO, prove to the world that you are real, let them see what I saw, what Darcey saw. Prove to them that I am not going mad, that we have not made this up and that you are a real person, entity, being, whatever you are, come forward."

His hands were visibly shaking, and I could see the tension in his eyes, it was as if he was asking for an end to this, like he was in pain. He was suffering, and it was my fault. I made my mind up straight away. I didn't want to see one of my closest friends feeling tormented like this, and before I'd even processed the thoughts, I noted the familiar feeling of all my cells igniting. Again, the glow surrounded my body as my clothes pixelated, transforming into iLUMiNO's purple and gold costume. I put my hand to my nose. I felt the straight ski slope nose of iLUMiNO. Flicking my hair with my hands, I had transformed into iLUMiNO.

Imagining the studio set, with the presenters Holly and Philip and Barkley, the transition began. From my living room, I could see a golden oval shape swirling right in front of me. This was different and very new to me. I'd not noticed this when I zoomed to Brighton or zoomed to the bike stand at work. Through the gold oval portal in my living room, I could see the presenters Holly and Philip, and Barkley, sat on the TV studio set's sofas. Still, instead of seeing what the camera was showing me on my TV set, I could see crew members, camera operators, in total, about fifteen people all stood in front of the studio set. Through the oval golden swarm of atoms, I focused on what I could see, and just as before, my vision zoomed in.

The studio's image appeared to open up, encompassing me like a fisheye lens surrounding me, and with a pop of pressure in my head and ears, just like being on a plane, I was in the studio.

The studio was in silence. No one said a word. I could hear the humming of the electricity from the high voltage lights, but that is all I heard. The two presenters sat but didn't speak; they were in just as much shock as the entire studio was.

I looked over at Barkley, and I smiled at him.

He looked like the weight of the world had lifted from his shoulders. His eyes lit up, as his smile filled his face.

I heard someone from the gallery or in the presenter's earpiece, shouting, "Say something, somebody for god sake say something!"

One of the producers on the studio floor shouted, "Geoff mic him up; quick!"

In his early twenties, a young man hurriedly ran up to me and clipped a lapel microphone onto the front of my costume. He unclipped the microphone receiver, a black box with a clip, from his belt where he had two other lapel microphones clipped into him. I guess if one of them failed during the live show; he was ready to switch microphones.

"I should clip this on you somewhere," he says looking at my cape and shaking his head, nervously he continued. Handing me the black microphone receiver, "Or you could always hold onto it."

I could hear a male voice deep in tone saying, "Cut the live feed. Cut the feed."

Across the studio floor was a tall man in a black suit. He looked out of place, compared to the crew who were all dressed casually in jeans, loose shirts, and some with baseball caps on.

I instantly assumed this to be the government or national security or whoever it was that had taken Barkley and Darcey.

"Do not cut this live show," I said as I walked over to the hosts Philip and Holly. They both stood up to greet me. Barkley remained seated. Three security men came bumbling into the studio out of breath, tasers in hand. The male presenter Philip saw them and shooed them back with his hand as he spoke into a camera.

"Let me address the viewers at home and explain what has just happened."

Holly held her hand out towards me, which I took ready to shake, but instead, she did a curtsy in front of me as if I was royalty.

Philip went straight into presenter mode and addressed a camera.

"Ladies and Gentleman, what you have just witnessed live on television is no computer trickery or special effects of any level. I can confirm complete honesty that what I have just seen here, along with this entire studio of about twenty people, and including you sat at home watching this right now, live on television, this man appeared out of thin air. From a golden plume of what looked like golden swirling steam, he stepped into our studio. This is breaking news, and this is live to the nation."

Philip turned around and faced me front on; he looked a lot smaller than I thought he would and had more wrinkles in the flesh.

"Please take a seat," he said. "Do we call you iLUMiNO? Is that your name?"

"Yes, my name is iLUMiNO," I said.

I turned to my left, Barkley was sitting on the edge of the sofa, placing my hand on his shoulder, I asked "Barkley, are you ok?"

He nodded and said, "Yes. Thank you so much for proving to the people that you are real. I was beginning to think that maybe you weren't. But, wow, I am... Just thank you, thank you for saving my life, and Darcey's too. Thank you."

Holly was transfixed on me, as if in a trance, "I'm sorry for staring," she said. "I just can't believe what I'm seeing, we've all seen the footage on the news, but I am..." she paused to think, "I don't know what I am, I guess I'm in some state of shock that you are real, and you're here."

Seeing Holly struggle to find the words, Philip took over. "I have to ask, I am sure there are a million questions to be asked. But the first one I have to ask, are you human? Are you from the future? Or are you using some new tech because what you have just demonstrated to us is not humanly possible and nor do we have the current technology to do so."

"Phillp, Holly, Barkley, and the viewers at home and across the world. I am human, and no, I am not from the future."

"Is there an explanation that we can understand as to how you can do what you can do? Are there more people like you with these abilities? Abilities such as flying, healing, moving objects like the gun. Should we be afraid? I can be honest and tell you and the viewers at home that I do not feel scared or threatened. I do, however, feel safe and..." he paused and then changed his voice to one of questioning himself, "I feel loved, if that makes sense, in your presence."

Holly agreed, "Yes, I feel precisely the same. I am in awe of your presence. You make me feel connected to myself. A loving that we all know to be true."

"Philip, to answer your questions. I do not have the full answers yet myself as to why I have these so-called powers, these abilities. However, I can tell you that I was part of a cosmic event that has somehow aligned my physical body with my spiritual and ethereal body, enabling me to have the abilities that I now have. I am still learning the extent of my abilities. In answer to your second question, no, there are no other people like me that I am aware of. I am an enigma to myself."

Holly smiled, "I would agree you are very enigmatic, but can I ask, why iLUMiNO? Do you have a real name? Do you go about life with normality? Do you have an alternate identity, or is this you? Is this you all of the time?"

Barkley took a real interest in this question, and he turned towards me in anticipation of the answer.

"I will be honest with you. As of right now, I still do have what I would call everyday life. One that doesn't include the abilities that I now possess. Whether that changes in the future who knows, but right now yes, I do have an alter ego."

Barkley sat back onto the sofa and relaxed a little.

Philip asked, "What is your purpose? Why are you here? Do you even know?"

"I am here to provide a balance of energies. To rid the earth of negative energy and to heal the earth. In doing so, enriching the earth to become a better place to be for all who inhabit it."

I didn't know where those words came from, but I believed in them wholeheartedly.

"I really must go now. I only came to alleviate Barkley's fears of my existence," I turned to Barkley before I stood up. "I am real, and I am as loyal to you now as I was when I removed that bullet from your shoulder. Positive thoughts, Barkley. Positive thoughts."

I imagined my living room, my golden aura illuminated, and in front of me the oval gold shape of swirling smoke and steam appeared, and like a pop my living room surroundings enveloped around me, and I was home. The golden aura was dissipating, and my purple and golden costume pixelated back to what I was wearing before.

The television was still on, and I was shocked to see that I was still in the studio due to the one-minute live television broadcast delay.

I watched it back as I turned across to Barkley. The words 'BREAKING NEWS LIVE' blazoned across the bottom of the screen.

I watched myself as I said to Barkley, "I am real, and I am as loyal to you now as I was when I removed that bullet from your shoulder. Positive thoughts, Barkley. Positive thoughts."

'iLUMiNO LIVE #POSITIVETHOUGHTS' replaced the Breaking News tag on the screen.

I watched on the television, and I could see the golden aura get more substantial and brighter around my body and then the smoke screen that was the golden oval appeared. In a flash, I disappeared along with the golden oval of swirling golden steam.

The studio camera cut to the two presenters; both looked dumbfounded.

Holly said, "Wow."

Philip replied, "Wow, indeed. You saw it, and you heard it here first."

He looked at the camera, and you could tell he was reading from an autocue, "Ladies and gentlemen, we are going to cut this programme short as we take you straight to the newsroom with breaking news just coming in. I've got a sneaky suspicion what it might be."

This was followed by a full screen breaking news card that filled the entire screen and the news bulletin theme.

The news presenter opened with, "We are sorry to interrupt your programming, but breaking news just in... The man who can fly, and saved Darcey Dyson from being shot, and saved Barkley Brown by removing a bullet from his shoulder leaving no trauma, has appeared live on television. iLUMiNO appeared out of nowhere during the live broadcast of the television show 'This Morning.'"

I turned the channels over, and each tv station was broadcasting 'Breaking News iLUMiNO is Real'.

That was it; I was indeed out in the public domain, I'd now made a pact with the citizens of my planet to make this world a better place, for all of us. I switched off the television, sat in my chair and smiled at myself.

iLUMiNO #positivethoughts. I liked it.

My phone rang. It was Barkley. "Where are you?" he asked.

"I'm at home. Why?"

"I'm in London, and the press is going mental on me. Have you seen what just happened live on TV?"

"No, what?" I lied.

"Oh man, you missed it, iLUMiNO appeared out of thin air while I was in the middle of this interview live on television. I'm on my way to the news studio now."

"What really? OMG, what happened?"

"Turn on the TV mate, you will see."

"Aaron, I have to go now, I'm being ushered into another studio. I need to go, they are telling me to turn off my mobile phone, but quick check, are we still on for this weekend's camping trip?"

"Sure, sure, I'll see you at my house, say 3 pm?"

"I'll be there."

THIRTEEN
Cliff Rescue

It was a colder night than had been forecast, and we were not expecting the rain. Just as we had finished pitching the tent, the heavens opened. Barkley ran from the car with our sleeping bags.

"I thought you said it was going to be a clear dry night," he shouted out to me as he slammed the boot of the car.

"That's what it said, I checked it twice, dry all night. It was forecast rain, but not until 10 am."

He came through the tent's zipper door with drops of rain permeating his jogger top and threw my sleeping bag at me. We had pitched our tent in the same place as last time; the tall tree behind us gave us a little shelter from the rain, but not a lot.

The rain formed mini streams, running down towards the bottom of the hill.

"Well, if this carries on, we won't be having a fire tonight." Barkley opened the cool box and pulled out his first can of beer. He pulled at the ring pull, and the gas released made the slow 'pssssssssch' sound. "I love that sound," he said as he took his first drink from the can.

"Pass me one," I said as he nearly emptied the can in one drink.

He threw one towards me and didn't say a word.

He had been reticent from picking me up at 3 pm. Usually, he would be talkative throughout the journey to wherever we were heading.

117

I opened my can of beer and took a sip from it. We both sat in silence and listened to the rain as it bounced off the sides of our tent.

I felt an unusual atmosphere that I had never experience with Barkley before. I looked at him but didn't feel the usual sense of calm that he brought me. I knew something about this situation was off. The atmosphere was different, thick, and full of cloudy intention.

"Come on, spit it out," I said. "There's something wrong, you've not said a word since you picked me up."

He looked across at me and took another swig from his can finishing what was left.

"Slow down mate. You'll make yourself sick."

He reached to the cool box, grabbed another can and opened it.

He looked at the open can until the froth had dissipated then looked across to me and shook his head.

"Have you and Kim had another fallout?" I said. "What over this time? You will be ok mate, you know you will, you two always make up afterwards."

He didn't say anything.

The stiff silence filled the tent. The rain continued to beat down on us. The tent door was still open, and you could see the rain bouncing off the floor.

I checked the weather app on my phone. Positively I said, "It's just a shower, it will pass over in five minutes or so."

"Good," came the reply. "I can't sit in here all night; I like to sit out in the camp chair and feel the outdoors."

Five minutes passed. The sound of the rain became quieter, and soon enough, the shower had passed.

Barkley jumped out of the tent and went straight to the car and pulled out two camp chairs. One was brand new with the tag still attached. He tore it off and looked over to me in the tent.

"Try not to flatten this one if you can help it!" his eyes twinkled, and a smile befell his face.

"I'll try not to."

I took the chair from him and shook it vigorously, which enabled it to open into position. We both sank into our chairs and opened another can of beer.

The ground was wet, and you could see a mist rising from the sodden grass.

The sun was nearly setting, and you could hear the remnants of the rain trickling off the plants and trees. The setting sun had cast an orange glow onto the water beads that had collected on the surrounding plants, and if you moved your head, they glistened and twinkled, reminding me of iLUMiNO's colours.

I looked over at Barkley, and he was admiring the colours too, either that or he was deep in thought.

"BB," I said. I waited until he returned from where he was in his head and made eye contact with me.

"Spill! Come on talk," I said.

"I'm ok," he said. "I've just had a lot to think about these last few weeks and..."

He petered off and didn't finish his sentence.

"Barkley, you are my longest, and one of my closest friends," I said. "We always talk things out and get things off our chest. That's how we roll. Whatever it is, let's talk through it mate."

He looked up to the sky, and I thought he was going to break down and cry. He took a big swig from his beer can. Squinting his eyebrows together, he slowly nodded as if he agreed with himself.

Looking over towards me and giving me direct eye contact, he said, "I know who iLUMiNO is."

I felt winded without any physical contact. I thought about how I was going to reply. What came out was a stutter as I tried to gasp for a breath, "Who..." I cleared my throat. "Who?" I said more confidently, appearing not to be that interested.

I sat and waited for his answer. As I did, I could feel my face getting hotter. I was sure I was turning red. Still, I didn't want to draw any added attention to myself, so I just took another drink from my can then pulled out my phone to distract any reaction I may or may not have been sending.

"It's you, Aaron. You are iLUMiNO."

He said it with such finesse and calmness. It was creepy, villainised by the coolness in his voice and the setting sun casting shadows across his eyes. He looked and sounded like a James Bond villain.

I spat my beer out, causing a spray all over my lap. Faking a laugh, I wiped my mouth and looked across at him. "No, really. Who do you think he is?"

"What's upsetting most is the fact that you didn't tell me and I had to find out for myself."

"You're serious right now? Please tell me you are joking," I said.

"Why didn't you trust me? Why couldn't you tell me, your best mate? If it were me, you would have been the first person I would have told."

"BB, you are proper barking up the wrong tree mate, I'm not iLU-MiNO," I nervously laughed. "I wish I was though. Imagine being able to do what he can do!"

I looked shameful as I replied, I felt so dishonest lying to my friend. I didn't want anyone to know, not even my best friend. I'm good at keeping secrets, especially about myself, but I've never been questioned or interrogated before. This is the first time I have had to lie about myself to a friend, and I felt guilty.

"You can drop the act, Aaron. It's ok. I get it. I get it all now. I just wished you would have told me instead of Darcey telling me."

"Darcey? Darcey Dyson?" I said, shocked and bewildered. How the hell would she know.

"What are you talking about Barkley. I'm not iLUMiNO, and as for Darcey Bastard Dyson, what does she know?"

"Darcey Bastard Dyson, eh! Someone seems upset," he said.

"Well, you're winding me up, and it's pissing me off. If I was iLU-MiNO, I could think of better things to do than sit here talking crap with you all night."

"Right then," he said, leaning forward, crushing his empty can and throwing it to the ground. "Look me directly in the eyes and tell me, you are not iLUMiNO, I want to hear it from you, I want you to swear on your parents grave that you are not iLUMiNO."

"Don't you dare bring my parents into this," I stood up and turned my back to him, shocked that Barkley would say this to me. No one has ever used my parents as a tool to get information from me, not even in jest.

"Aaron, sit down, I didn't mean to mention your parents. I'm sorry. I'm just angry, I guess, that I found out from someone else."

"Angry," I said, turning around. "Barkley listen to me, I am not iLU-MiNO, and whatever information Darcey has got is wrong." My voice was intense and raised. I sat down, throwing myself back into the camp chair taking a long drink from my can. "How on earth did she come to this conclusion then? Go on, do tell. I think I am going to find this story rather interesting." My voice had changed to patronising. Barkley did not seem fazed at all.

"All right then I'll tell you," he said.

"There are some loose ends granted, but if you connect all the dots, they all point to you. I'll start with Leigh."

"Leigh, what's she got to do with this?"

"Leigh told me she saw a man floating outside the hospital ward window at work one morning."

"She's told me this story too. We decided that she must have been seeing things."

"She also told me she felt for sure it was you. The floating man didn't look like you, but she was sure as hell it was you."

"I can't believe she told you that. She told me not to tell anyone in fear of her going mad."

"It didn't mean anything until the day of the shooting."

"The day of the shooting?"

"The day iLUMiNO showed up for the first time."

I knew where this was heading, but I let him continue. I was listening with a knowledge of how and what happened, but with an expression of intrigue.

"When iLUMiNO extracted the bullet from my shoulder. I looked directly into his eyes and saw you. I had a knowing, a feeling, a connectedness, that only friends of thirty eight years would know. I saw you, Aaron, I saw you. When I got back into the coffee shop, you said the exact words that iLUMiNO said to me. I can still hear you saying it now. 'What were you thinking.'"

"You've already told me this at Leigh's party," I said flippantly.

"Ok right yeah, fair enough," he said.

"Is that it? Is that your compelling evidence that makes me without question iLUMiNO?"

"Then there was the appearance at the TV Studios."

I glanced at him wearily wondering where he was going with this.

"Go on then," I said mockingly, "What did I supposedly do live on television that outed myself as me being iLUMiNO?"

"So iLUMiNO appeared out of thin air, from an oval shape of golds and yellow mist right in front of our eyes."

"Ok right, yeah, you called me straight after remember, and I watched it back on the news. It's still dominating all the news now, and that was more than a week ago."

"Well, when he..." he corrected himself. "When you came up and sat next to me live on television. I knew it was you; I knew it was you because that's what friends do when they're needed."

"BB, you are deluded mate. Honest to god, I have never heard so much babble come out of your mouth before. I think this iLUMiNO fellow has got under your skin..."

He cut me off, "And when it was time for you to leave, you stepped back into the golden mist..."

"Barkley for the last time I am not iLUMiNO, what do I have to do to spell it out..."

"And before the portal closed, I could see the silver picture frame of your folks on their wedding day on your sideboard. You know the one with the ornate corners."

Barkley held his hand to his chin gently stroking it; now he really did look like a villain from a James Bond movie.

"What?" I squealed. "Come on, I've never heard anything as ridiculous! What the... I mean... Really? Come on, mate, you must have been seeing things, surely, think about it."

"Oh, I have thought about it. I have thought about it a lot."

"Mate, you have lost the plot." I reached into the cool box and grabbed us both a beer and threw him a can over and said, "And what's this got to do with Darcey Dyson?"

"Oh Darcey, well she was able to get me the footage to prove I didn't see things. You see, having a journalist as your friend can come in useful."

"Friend? She's no friend of yours, she is only out for one thing."

"And what's that?"

"Fame, getting to the top."

Barkley pulled the ring pull from his can, "If you'll let me finish. So, she did a bit of digging and..."

"Digging!" I snapped. "Is that what you call it, digging around."

"It's what she does, Aaron, she's a reporter."

"So, after doing some digging," he continued, "she managed to get the CCTV footage from inside the coffee shop on the day of the shooting."

"And?" I quickly sniped back at him.

"Well, it turns out you didn't hide behind the upturned tables with the rest of the customers during the shooting at all. You went into the toilets."

"I don't see what you are getting at here; if I was in the toilets or behind the tables, so what! Does it matter? All I know is I wanted to get out of the way."

"Then there is an unusually bright flash of light that comes out of the toilet door. Just a few seconds after you had entered them."

"A camera glare, a glitch, it could be anything."

"It just so happens that when iLUMiNO flies off from the shooting scene, seconds later, there is another flash coming from the toilets, and then out walks Aaron, and you crouch behind the table as if you have been there all along."

"You are off your head mate, really, come on, think about it. I mean, think about it. Everything you're saying is circumstantial, coincidental."

"What about the photo frame of your mum and dad? I saw it, Aaron, with my own eyes."

"I watched the TV show back. You told me to when you called me up remember? So, I watched the entire episode on catch up, as you asked. Now do you remember before your interview, there was a section on photography, wasn't there? And the presenter had a display of fifteen photo frames of varying sizes. It could have been one of those that you saw through the fog. Think about it Barkley, think about how this looks from my point of view."

Barkley slumped back in his chair, undefeated. "Well, Darcey is in the middle of obtaining the footage from every camera that was in that studio. Six studio cameras and eight security cameras; she is sure to find something. I don't understand why you just can't tell me, after all the evidence, and you still deny it to your best mate." He stood up, took a long drink from his can, threw it onto the ground and headed off into the woods.

"Where are you going?" I asked.

"I'm going for a walk. I need to clear my head," he said.

I decided to leave him be and let him cool down for a while. I knew it wouldn't be too long before he came back.

I decided to call Leigh.

Unlocking my phone, I selected favourites and clicked on Leigh's name.

She answered after the third ring, "What's up?"

"What do you mean, 'What's up?'" I replied laughing, "Your best pal decides to call you, and the first thing you ask is 'what's up'? How rude," I continued to laugh.

"Pal," she said. "You barely ever ring, it's always a text, so I'm privileged, thank you. So, I'll ask again," she continued, "what's up?"

"No, nothing really. I'm on one of our getaway camping trips with Barkley, currently sat in a folding camp chair on the top of Tinketropy Quarry."

"What are you doing up there? You'll get yourself killed."

"We've been coming here months. It's ok, we got a lovely spot, it's relatively peaceful."

"So come on, what's up? You keep diverting my question. Where's Barkley? say 'hey' from me."

I didn't say anything; I just let the silence fill the phone.

"Aaron, are you there?"

"He's gone for a walk," I replied. "He's gone to let off some steam."

"Has this got anything to do with the fact that he thinks you're that iLUMiNO geezer?"

"How did you kn..."

She cut me off before I could finish my sentence.

"At the party, he asked me about anything strange happening lately. Especially if it involved you."

"Me?"

"I know, right? Anyway, the only thing I could think of was that time when I saw that man floating out of the window at work."

"You told me to draw a line under that and never to repeat it, in case someone thought you were going mad."

"Well yeah", she paused "but that was before this iLUMiNO character turned up and saved the day flying all around Redgrand."

"And why did you tell him about your vision and that it was connected to me?"

"Well, he asked me, didn't he. He said if anything strange had happened with you. So I just told him about the floating man thing. I told him that he didn't look like you, to be fair, I can't remember what he looked like now, to be honest. But, although he didn't look like you, I had a feeling, like a knowing that it was you. Weird, very weird still to this day. It was like a dream inside a dream. Aaron, I'll never get over it."

"He has got it into his head that I am iLUMiNO and we've just had a right fall out over it. He'll calm down though."

"Oooh, lovers tiff hey," her raucous laugh billowed from my phone.

Our conversation moved to other things. She was well settled in now at the apartment. She was excited to tell me about applying for promotion to Junior Ward Sister.

"Great," I said. Realising the time, I quickly rounded off the conversation. I had realised that I had drunk three cans of beer, and nearly an hour had passed. We arranged to meet up next week for a coffee.

"Listen, I'm going to go now. I'll try to ring Barkley. He's been gone for nearly an hour. I think he will have calmed down by now."

"No problem sugar tits," she said, "I'll see you next week," and hung up.

My phone's home screen illuminated my face. I scrolled back to my favourites button and selected BB and pressed the call button. Almost immediately, his phone lit up, and I could hear his ringtone. The superman theme tune rang out, and his camping chair lit up. He had left his phone on the chair.

"Barkley," I moaned as I hung up. I stood up and took a look around, wondering if he was lingering nearby. There was no sign of him.

I remembered that he also had a burner phone. Quickly I went into my phone's contacts and scrolled to 'BB Temp'. Again I clicked the call button, and then I heard the old fashioned ringer coming from the tent.

"Thank God," I thought. "He's in the tent!" I pulled the nylon screen back, and the tent was empty. His burner phone was ringing from inside his jacket. Hanging up, I took the burner phone and his other phone from the camp chair, put them in my coat, and set off in the direction he left me.

FOURTEEN
Coming Out... Again!

I'd been walking through the trees and undergrowth for about twenty minutes. It was dark, very dark, I kept shouting out 'Barkley' every so often, but nothing. I could hear the trees rustle. There was a light breeze, and the mist was rising from the quick shower that we had had earlier. It looked like the set of a horror movie, quite majestical, like the area had a life of its own, but I couldn't appreciate the beauty as I was worried about Barkley.

"Barkley!" I continued to shout, but nothing, no reply. It got darker the further I roamed, and I had to use the torch function on my phone.

The light shone just enough for me to see the ground.

I stood still and listened. 'Barkley!" I shouted again.

Nothing.

I took stock of what was unfolding and wondered to myself if I should use some of my abilities. The conundrum was difficult. Do I use my abilities to find Barkley and risk the fact that he may see me, threatening a more profound fallout exposing the truth that I have been lying to him? Or not?

I kept on searching and shouting. My phone beeped. Low battery. Then it turned itself off. After my eyes had adjusted to the darkness, I could see the moonlight breaking through the tree branches, giving me some vision of where to go. I cupped my hand to my mouth hoping to throw my voice further. 'Barkley' again I shouted. Again nothing. I was beginning to get worried and was feeling mad at him for just walking off like that.

The trees began to thin out and open up, more light from the moon started to brighten up the ground, I could see the dark green shades of grass, and undergrowth reflecting the moonlight back up at me, giving me a clearer vision of what was in front of me. In the distance though, this disappeared into blackness, pure blackness, like looking out to sea. I slowly walked towards what was the edge of the old quarry cliff.

Looking down into the abyss, I shouted his name again, "Barkley!" Again, no reply. I lowered myself to the ground to get a better look. The cliffside had varying levels cut into the rock. Even falling from the first level would cause serious injury. My worry soon turned into fear. I feared the worst.

I could feel the cells of my body beginning to ignite; it was an un-conscious decision. I had started to change into iLUMiNO. The gold-en aura started to appear, but as soon as it did, I saw Barkley's boots to the left of me on the next level of the cliff edge. I moved to the left of the cliff edge and saw Barkley laid out on his front, with his head tilted to one side. I could see he was breathing. My cells relaxed, and the or-ange glow that had started dissipated. He had sustained a cut to his left eyebrow; I could just about see his injury.

"Barkley!" I shouted. He moaned, and there was some slight move-ment from his legs. "I'm coming, mate. You're ok, do not move."

He was right on the edge and if he moved too far to the right he would be over the cliff edge, which was considerably higher than the fall he'd just had. I began to lower myself down the cliffside; it was ap-proximately two stories to the level that Barkley was on. By placing my feet strategically on the jagged edges that were chiselled into the rock, I slowly lowered myself down. It took five minutes of careful manoeu-vring. I wish I could have just flown down.

Finally, I got to the bottom and rolled him into the recovery position away from the edge. "BB," I said and shook his shoulder. "BB, wake up, you've had a fall."

He moaned and attempted to say my name, but ended up coughing. He opened his eyes and looked up at me. The wound to his head was open but didn't look that deep, it would only require a paper stitch. The blood had congealed and was no longer actively bleeding.

"Aaron," he said, "Thank god." He was still in the recovery position as he gained more consciousness. "I need iLUMiNO," he said. "Help me."

I sharply answered back, "There is no frigging iLUMiNO. Now get up we need to get you to a hospital."

He looked at me transfixed and looked at my hands, and clothes, he could see that I had climbed down the rock face to get to him.

He sat up, slowly groaning with pain as he did. He bent his knees and held his hand to his open wound.

"Have you broken anything?" I asked, "Have you hurt yourself anywhere else?"

He shook his head, "I don't think so."

He tried to stand but went dizzy and sat back down as fast as he had stood.

"You're concussed," I said, looking up to the clifftop. "We need to get back up there. Do you think you can do it?"

He looked up and said, "Give me five minutes mate. I'll be ok."

Barkley's burner phone rang from the inside of my jacket. Only Darcey Dyson and myself had the number.

I handed it to him. He looked at the caller's number and hung up.

The cliffside was still wet from the downpour earlier, and although it looked slippy, it was relatively easy to grip onto and climb up. Barkley went first. I gave him my back to stand on as he made the first step. He began to climb, knocking gravel down into my face. He managed a couple of metres, and he looked down at me, "Can you do it?"

"I'm good," I said. "Keep going."

Barkley got to the top and looked down at me. I hadn't moved. I wasn't able to get a good grip. I needed some height to grab the first piece of rock that jutted out. I needed someone's back to stand on, or I just needed to fly, but neither of them was going to happen.

"Barkley", I shouted up. "I can't reach that rock. I'm stuck. I need some rope or something."

"Hang on," he said. "I've got a tow rope in the car."

Twenty minutes later I heard an out of breath Barkley puffing and panting, "Aaron, are you still there?"

"Yeah," I shouted up.

"Here grab on to this and tie it around your waist."

He threw down a yellow rope with a metal clip at the end; I hooked it around my waist and held onto it with both hands.

"Ready," I shouted. "Pull."

The rope went taut as he began to pull. I placed my feet in front of me and started walking up the cliff face as Barkley pulled. It wasn't long before I could see his feet as I got nearer to the top.

The rope stopped. I was no longer being pulled. Barkley looked down at me, I could see he had work gloves on, and the rope was tight around his hands.

"Why have you stopped? Come on I am nearly there."

He looked at me. His eyes were penetrating the back of my skull.

"Promise me now you are not iLUMiNO," he said, his voice beginning to crack.

I looked back at the cliff edge beneath me and looked further into the darkness, "What? Come on, stop messing about, just one more pull and I'm up," I said.

His eyes began to water. He was getting upset, and his hands began to shake as he said. "If I let go I will know for certain one way or another if you are iLUMiNO."

"Barkley," I said. "If you let go and I don't make it, you will have to live with that for the rest of your life." My eyes started to fill with tears too, "Barkley look at me, I climbed down here to get you, you were unconscious, for all I knew you were dead. Don't you think if I was iLU-MiNO that I'd have done something easier like use my so-called powers to rescue you, or have flown down? Think about it!"

There was a small silence while he processed what I said.

"Look at me. I am here now, my life in your hands. Do you want to take this risk with me? Your best pal, your longest pal? Is that what my life means to you?" Another awkward silence filled the air as he contemplated. "Just pull me up goddamnit, Barkley. Please, I'm begging you!"

He could see my eyes were filled with tears, and my voice was panicked, filled with desperation.

"You're begging me?" he said to himself.

"You're begging me," he repeated and then it was as if lightning had struck and he realised the situation he found himself in.

"Oh mate, I am so sorry," he said as he began to pull. "Jesus, what was I thinking?"

I got closer to the top, and he grabbed my hand and pulled me to the ground.

I just sat there on the ground, wiped the beads of sweat from my forehead, and laughed.

I don't know what I was laughing for. Maybe I was glad that Barkley didn't let go, or perhaps I was laughing at myself for completing my first scene as an actor. A scene that Beulah Big Tits as Leigh calls her would have been proud of. What if Barkley would had let go of me? I don't know if I would have faked an injury or revealed myself as iLUMiNO. Either way, I was delighted with my acting debut. The only negative was that I felt bad for lying to Barkley.

Heading back to the tent, we didn't say much. The moon was higher in the sky now and gave good vision on the ground.

Back at base, Barkley slid onto his camp chair and I got a plaster out of the first aid box from the car. I stuck it on the wound above Barkley's eye.

He looked up at me and said, "I've been a prick. I'm sorry."

He grabbed two beers from the cool box and threw one at me.

"I honestly believed that there was something you weren't telling me. I've known you nearly all my life, and I just had this knowing, this feeling. I guess it overtook me. I'm sorry mate. Honestly, I am."

"But we all have secrets, don't we?" I looked across at him from my camp chair.

"What do you mean? I don't have any secrets from you at all, I never have." He paused and took a drink, then rested the can on his knee.

He looked over at me and quietly asked, "Is there something you want to tell me, Aaron?"

I looked back at him and took a deep breath.

"I'm gay, ok. There you have it," I said, "I am gay!"

FIFTEEN
London Bound

I stood in my kitchen the very next day, a huge mug of coffee in hand, staring out into my garden. I immediately felt calm as I looked out into my own little piece of paradise. I cast my mind back to Barkley on our camping trip. I'd never anticipated telling him I was gay but it seemed easier than telling him I was this iLUMiNO guy who was popping up all over the place. I'm sure that Barkley knew who I truly was, both my sexuality and my 'superhero' identity, but he was kind enough just to focus on my confession. It wasn't that I'd expressly hidden the fact I was gay, not exactly, anyway. I just hadn't 'come out' to people. God, I hated that phrase. But I'd just never found the right time to tell him. I'm sure it hurt him immensely that I'd kept this a secret for so long, we were best friends, after all. He was the closest thing I had to family. I keep playing it over in my mind.

"Okay then," was all he'd said. It wasn't a big deal to him. It was just who I was. We'd fallen back into an easy bickering afterwards about God only knew what and that was that. It was over. Nothing had changed. Things were completely back to normal. Gulping the remnants of my coffee, I climbed the stairs to bed, preparing for my night-shift that evening. I always drank a mug of strong coffee before bed, it allowed me to wake-up feeling somewhat awake ready for the hopefully steady shift ahead of me.

I was in the canteen when my phone beeped with a text. Barkley. Did I want to go and watch his interview at the news desk studios where Darcey works? Of course, I did! It was my chance to taste the high life, as close as I'd ever come to the glitz and glamour of Hollywood. Stuffing my phone back into my pocket, I finished the rest of my shift with a grin on my face, excited to be invited backstage with Barkley. It wasn't until I was climbing into bed that morning, that I began to feel uneasy about the whole thing. Not only was there the party-line that Barkley had strongly been suggested to follow during his interviews, which made me feel scared that something more sinister was afoot with this whole superhero thing I'd gotten myself into. But the fact that Darcey and Barkley had become so pally left me with a pit in my stomach. Barkley wasn't necessarily one of those people who became friends with everybody, but somehow Darcey had weaselled her way into his trust through nothing more than a shared experience. There was something about her that I just didn't like. I couldn't put my finger on it. As I fell into a deep sleep, I dreamed of soaring over the rooftops of my hometown.

The next week went in a flash and before I had time to think too deeply into the iLUMiNO situation, I was travelling down to London with Barkley ready for the interview. It was a big deal, a really big deal, and would be filmed prior to it airing, Piers Morgan style, with two chairs facing each other in a posh-looking suite-style room. It was a huge deal. We were in high spirits on the train down, the news studio had sprung for First Class seats and we were making the most out of the waiter service, both having drunk a few beers (in ice-cold glasses). I could have gotten there much faster, of course, but that wouldn't do me any favours right now. Plus, I wanted to spend more time with Barkley anyway. We spent the rest of the day taking in the sights of London before heading back to the hotel, completely gratis thanks to the news company, ready for the next day when Barkley would be filming his interview.

Walking the towering streets of London made me feel very small and inconsequential. The lights glistened against the cobblestoned pavement. Feeling merry from our day, we decided to have one final pint in a pub just around the corner of the hotel. Metropolis was a hole-in-the-wall pub, a commuter hang-out bar built under the railway arches with cask ales, pub menu and looked just as inviting as the local pubs back home. But, this is London, and London is known for being nothing if not a bit bougie. Entering through the oak door, I was transported back in time into an old-fashioned library. It was still a pub, predominantly, but the walls were lined with old hardback books. Newspapers lined the remaining walls and the tables were made from old type-writers. Glancing at Barkley for the go-ahead, we walked inside and found a seat opposite each other on a baroque desk. After drinking a pint (or two) I headed to the toilet, unable to hold my bladder until we were back at the hotel. As I zigzagged through the crowd a feeling overcame me. Complete unease. That's when I saw it. The emergency exit was propped open showing an alleyway steeped in darkness. On the floor was a woman covered in blood, atop her was a man attempting to hike her skirt above her head. Without thinking, I morphed into my alter-ego, as I ran towards them.

"Leave the woman alone. Get off her!" I snarled at the man. He took one look at me and his face cracked into a smile. "Aren't you the one from TV?" He laughed, standing up and peeling himself from the woman, who immediately shuffled back against the wall and curled into a ball.

"Get out of here, now!" I bit, running towards him, hoping I wouldn't actually have to fight him. I wasn't much of a fighter truth be told, but if that was what it took to keep this woman safe, then I would do it.

"Alright man, I'm going. She's not worth it anyway!" He turned and ran, clearly intimidated but not wanting to show it. But my job wasn't done yet. I turned to the woman on the floor, mascara tracks traced the lines down her face.

"Thank you," she said as I walked over to her.

"Are you okay? Did he hurt you?" I hoped my meaning was clear, I didn't want to ask anything too personal as she was already in a state.

"No, he didn't. I'm sure he would have if you hadn't seen us." She smiled and tried to stand, grasping her side and wincing. "I think when he pushed me down, I banged my side on the wall, that's all. I'll be okay."

"Can I see? I might be able to help?" I was amazed that this woman hadn't commented on my outfit, or the fact that I did glow an ethereal gold.

"Sure," she slid her top up on one side, showing an already blossoming bruise. I placed my hand upon it, checking her eyes for permission. I breathed in and out slowly, willing the pain away. Even as the pain in her side dissipated, I could sense that there was pain elsewhere. Not physical, but mental. The scars from being attacked went much deeper than a physical bruise, it was something that could haunt a person forever. I'd seen it in my job one too many times.

I reached forwards, placing my index finger right where your third eye would be. Just above the brows and nose, at the centre of the forehead. I closed my eyes and felt the pain. I felt that it would fester within her over the years, growing and becoming something far more sinister. As I breathed out, I felt the pain leaving her. I knew right in that moment, that this event wouldn't affect this woman as it once would have. She'd be able to go on and be happy, without the mental scars from this attack.

"Woah," she said as I removed my hand. "What did you do?"

"I healed you," I said with no hint of irony. "Now, please do report him. You can't let him get away with that."

"I will, I promise! Thank you iLUMiNO. I can't believe that I met you in person."

"You're welcome. Now, go home through the front of the bar. Get straight into a taxi and stay safe," I said as I slipped back into the toilets morphing back into my regular clothes. It had been a close call. I could feel power buzzing within me. It seemed that I became stronger the more I used my powers. I hoped that I hadn't been too long and that Barkley wouldn't ask too many questions about where I'd been. It turned out that I needn't have worried. When I returned from the toilet, Barkley was chatting to the buxom blonde barmaid looking pretty happy with himself. I smiled knowing that my friend, despite everything, was still my friend and very, very happy.

Barkley's interview went without a hitch. He looked very dapper in his suit sitting across from Jamie Olsen, one of the biggest journalists in the world, who had flown in from America just to speak to him. iLUMiNO was big news, a global phenomenon , and every major news station were vying to get an interview with Barkley and Darcey, preferably at the same time, but either/or was better than nothing. Darcey's career had sky-rocketed and she was so busy that there was no way she could possibly attend every interview requested of her. As luck would have it, she was able to attend this one. She sat by my side as Barkley smiled and recounted his story to Jamie Olsen, nodding occasionally when Barkley said something particularly inspired. When Barkley finished, it was Darcey's turn in the spotlight. She quite literally effervesced with energy, clearly loving every ounce of attention she was given. Once the filming interviews were in the can, we all met in the hotel restaurant for lunch. During this time the producer would look over the footage and then Barkley and Darcey would reshoot anything they needed before declaring it a wrap. I didn't understand why so many interviews were necessary, since they said the same things every time, but it wasn't my place to say anything. Plus, I liked being along for the ride.

After cramming our plates full of buffet food and picking a table to sit at, Darcey came over to join us.

"Hello boys!" Despite her maturity, she was such a flirt. Darcey had the ability to make any man do anything she wanted, and she milked it. "Are you going to top up your coffee Aaron?" she fluttered her eyelids at me, impervious to the fact that her 'charms' wouldn't work on me. She was far from my type.

"Not just yet," I smiled in response.

"I'll grab you some," a member of staff, who had quite obviously been listening to our conversation, said, grabbing Darcey's cup.

"Thank you, darling," Darcey said, her hand lingering slightly too long on the young man's.

Darcey turned her attention to me. "I heard about Barkley's little accident on your camping trip. You saved his life, didn't you?"

"That's a bit of a stretch. I wouldn't say I saved him. He saved himself!" I tried to joke but Darcey was having absolutely none of it.

"Oh he definitely saved me," Barkley said through a mouthful of sandwich. "Az is too modest!"

"How lucky he was, that you got there just there in the nick of time. So lucky," Darcey drawled.

"I'm not sure what you mean," I answered, feeling unnerved by the line of questioning. There was no way she could know who I was. Absolutely none, but yet that seemed to be what she was hinting at.

"Oh, I think you do," Darcey said. I looked to Barkley to see how he was taking all of this. He was far too busy stuffing the sandwich into his face to even realise I was being interrogated. He'd never been one for social cues.

"No idea, Darcey. How's that coffee?" I asked, trying to change the subject.

"Gorgeous," Darcey said, taking the coffee off the young boy who'd just returned to our table. "I actually think I'll take this in my room. I do have some footage to review. I'm determined to find out who our friend iLUMiNO is. Our kind friends at This Morning have sent over the footage for me to review. Isn't that kind of them!"

As Darcey was standing up, she turned to us both and said, "I have two spare tickets to the new Keanu Reeves film if you boys would like to join me. Keanu is now a good friend of mine, and I'd love for you to meet him. He's as handsome in real life," she said winking at me.

"Yes, we'd love to! Wouldn't we Az!" Barkley smiled up at Darcey Dyson.

"Sure, thank you," I said. Not knowing how to respond to the situation. It looked like I was going to be attending film premieres with A-List actors from now on. What a turn of events.

I eyed Darcey as she shimmied out of the room. There was something off about her. The only way I could get to the bottom of it was to spend more time with her. God, I wish I was back in my beautiful zen garden!

SIXTEEN
As You Are

Feeling the need to tidy, as I always did when I was thinking, I climbed into the attic and decided to clear out some of the old boxes I'd stuffed up there when I moved in. Cleaning and tidying was my process. It helped me through problems I was facing. Currently, in my life, there were two main problems. Darcey, and the fact that I was iLUMiNO. I had no idea how this would fit into my life. I was just a hospital porter, who happened to love his job, and his life if truth be told. iLUMiNO didn't fit into my plans for a normal life. Thoughts of Darcey, the upcoming film premiere, and iLUMiNO filled my brain as I threw old, broken items into a bin bag. As I worked my way to the back of the room, I came across a box I hadn't seen before. Or at the very least, one I couldn't remember. It was a ratty, cardboard box, the kind you buy when you're moving house. Sliding the other boxes out of the way, I crawled across the loft-boards and pulled the box towards me. My heart stopped when I realized what was written on the side. In my mum's delicate looping handwriting, in black marker pen, was written 'misc. items'.

After getting over the initial surprise of seeing my mum's handwriting, I peeled the lid off the box, not entirely sure of what to expect. There were various ornaments that I recognized from our living room, some paperwork, and then, at the very bottom of the pile, was a photo-album. My mum and dad were the kind of people who documented everything they could with a camera. They had photographs all around the house, many of which I now have around my house, but I hadn't seen this album before. I didn't recognise it all. The pale blush covers were plain, without any decoration at all. I turned the cover back, revealing the first page. There was me, as a young baby, a very young baby, swaddled in a white Redgrand hospital blanket. Had I mentioned that I was born there too?

Flipping each page took me through the years of my own life. In the kitchen sink having a bath, my first day of nursery, our holidays to Skegness, me with my grandparents, my friends, and various family members. There were a few pictures of mum and dad dotted sporadically throughout the pages, but it was mostly me. I was in every single photograph. The last one was me in my care home scrubs holding up my brand-new driving licence. It had come in the post when I returned home from work and my mum was so excited that I hadn't been allowed to change before she took the photo. They were always proud of me, no matter what I did. I felt a twinge of happiness at that. Bittersweet, but happy, nonetheless.

The pages fell open onto the back page of the photo album. At this moment, not one thought of anything other than my wonderful parents crossed my mind. I was totally and completely in the moment. As I went to close the final page, a slip of yellowing paper fell out from between the slip-cover. Written in biro was a poem. My dad's handwriting this time graced the pages. In the low light of the attic, I couldn't quite make out the words. Climbing back down the ladder, my hand shaking as I did so, I grasped the paper tightly. I sat at the very top of the stairs, holding the piece of paper in front of my face, and started to read.

As You Are
My son, my only child. I love you more each day than
the last.
The breath I breathe is for you.
The love I give is for you.

Your mother and I
know what makes you you. We know what makes you
special.
Aaron, I hope that one day you can
be who you are. Truly and unashamedly who you are.
Who you love doesn't matter to us.
I pray that you are happy and
satisfied.
A life well-lived, with the right man.
We've known all along, my child and
know you will tell us in your own time. So
when that time arrives, we will simply share this
poem and you will know that you are loved
as you are.
Wholly as you are.
As you are.

I had to read the poem through a couple of times before the message could really sink in. The words were written by a true Redgrand man. The kind of man who wouldn't readily share any feelings for fear of looking weak and unmanly. Tears streamed down my own face as the meaning seeped into me. My parents had known all along that I was gay. And it didn't matter to them in the slightest. The words my dad had painstakingly written in his typical 'dad' handwriting meant more to me than anything else in the world. I was accepted, truly accepted by my parents. The date etched into the top corner of the page, just like you would at school, said Thursday 31st July 1997. The day they died. My dad, likely accompanied by my mum, would have written this on the morning of my 21st birthday. I'd thought the car would have been a pretty amazing gift, but nothing could top this. They'd give it to me when I was ready to tell them and then I'd know that everything was okay.

I'm not sure how much time I spent sitting there, re-reading the page over and over again. When my phone buzzed in my pocket, it was like I'd awoken from a trance. The screen illuminated with a message from Leigh asking if she could come around for a coffee. I know for a fact that she'd sent the message as a courtesy and was likely already on her way over here, so I couldn't say no. After the rollercoaster of emotions I'd felt, I didn't know whether I could bring myself to tell Leigh about the letter, and that I was gay. She'd know that something was wrong straight away, she always did. I'd get that motherly look and spill whatever was troubling me. I always did.

Leigh walked straight in through the front door shouting that she was here. Not that you could possibly miss her, she was like a whirlwind. Loud and proud. Slamming the door shut behind her, she called out asking where I was.

"Garden," I shouted back. Knowing that she'd arrive minutes after she texted, I'd already got a pot of coffee ready and gone to sit outside. The grey rattan furniture set made me feel like I was in Ibiza, even if the Redgrand weather wasn't quite up to snuff. As I poured Leigh a coffee into the largest mug I owned, (she was a coffee addict like me). She threw herself down into a chair and sighed.

"What's up, pal?" I asked, pushing the coffee mug in her direction.

"I have something to confess..." Leigh edged. It was clear from her voice that she was worried about my reaction to whatever news she was about to tell me.

"Confess your sins," I laughed, trying to make her feel at ease. I don't remember the last time I'd seen her look nervous. She was always the confident, life of the party type.

"Okay, well, I'm pregnant," Leigh gritted her teeth and smiled, waiting for my reaction.

"Leigh, oh my god! Congratulations!" I shouted as she broke into a true smile. "You are happy about it, aren't you?" I double-checked before I launched into a tirade about how good a mother she'd be.

"Yes, I'm so happy. We're so happy. I just can't quite believe it. I did like fifteen tests, just to make sure. But, yeah, I'm going to be a mum!"

"Oh Leigh, I'm so happy for you!" I gushed, lunging across the table and wrapping her into a hug.

Baby talk consumed us for the next hour or so. Did she want a boy or girl? Boy. Did she want to breast-feed or bottle-feed? Bottle-feed. And so on. As she stood up to leave, I asked to feel the baby. It was too soon, I knew that. But I couldn't help myself. As I cupped the gentle slope of her stomach, I felt the most overwhelmingly pure power within her. I could see it in front of me, a completely white light emanating from Leigh's belly. It was stronger than anything I'd ever felt before, new and untapped potential. And my best friend was bringing it into the world. I could tell the baby was happy and healthy. I secretly thanked iLUMiNO for the power to see within Leigh, to feel the energy that she was bringing into the world. It felt spectacular. She smiled at me as I peeled my hands away.

"Feel anything?" She joked, knowing full well I wouldn't.

"I definitely felt the baby kick," I laughed.

"That would be the burrito I had earlier, sorry!"

With that, we both descended into belly laughs.

"I have to go now, Az! Stop making me laugh!" Leigh screeched as she walked back through the patio doors and into the kitchen. "What's that?"

I turned my head to see what she was pointing at. The poem. Before I could explain, she'd already picked it up and begun to read.

"Your dad?" was all she said, her voice barely more than a whisper.

"Yes," I nodded, not knowing what else to say. Unusual for me!

"They knew you were gay? And they accepted you. Az, that's amazing news, right? That's got to feel amazing, hasn't it?" Leigh reached out and placed a hand on my arm.

"Wait, you knew?" I managed to choke out.

"Of course, I did," Leigh left the sentence hanging before me.

"Why didn't you tell me you knew?" I asked.

"Because it didn't make any difference to me," Leigh pulled me into a hug. Once again, I felt the energy pulsating inside her belly as it pushed against me. Leigh would be a great mother. I was sure of it.

SEVENTEEN
Sixth Sense

After trying, and failing, to fit into my old suit I gave up and went shopping. It was the day before the big movie premiere and I'd, somewhat mistakenly, presumed that I'd fit into the suit I'd worn for years. I wasn't fat, or overweight, but my suit button no longer fastened in the middle, due to the muscles: my abs, I actually had some abs, and I'd filled out a bit. Plus, the extra slices of cake I'd been having with my coffee probably hadn't helped. If I was going to be meeting the one and only Keanu Reeves, then there was no way I was squashing myself into a suit that didn't fit.

You would think that as a 'superhero', I'm not sure what to call myself but superhero seems to be the only thing that fits, I'd have rock-hard Ryan Gosling type abs; well, they are on their way, but I still look exactly like myself. Rather normal, some muscle taking shape, but still pretty regular. Barkley was joining me on the trip to Talon Hall, our local shopping centre, not that he needed a new suit. He'd bought some new ones recently thanks to his new fame. He'd agreed to give me the honest truth about which suit would look best on the red carpet, and possibly catch the eye of a super-rich, super hot celebrity or two. That was how I came to be standing in the middle of the Top Man changing rooms, with blue cigarette trousers, brown shoes, and a white shirt. I had to admit that I looked pretty damn good. Grown-up, even though as a forty-something, I was well-aware I was grown up. There's nothing like a new suit to make you feel like an adult!

"I think you need to choose one of these jackets," Barkley said, looking to the sullen teenage salesgirl for confirmation. She grunted in assent and thrust one of the jackets towards me.

"I thought I might skip the jacket. Doesn't it look a bit more modern without one?" I asked tentatively. I was usually giving fashion advice to others, it was rare that I was ever on the receiving end.

"No, you need a jacket," the salesgirl said as she popped her chewing gum.

Not wanting to disappoint, I slid into the blue jacket. It fit nicely, tailored at the waist. As I was admiring myself, she threw a tie from behind me. I caught it as it came for my face, something I likely wouldn't have been able to do before iLUMiNO came along. I'd been noticing things like that for the past few days. Little things that are seemingly normal to the folk around me, but they strike me as odd. For example, my sense of smell has heightened. And I get the strangest sensation that I can intuit what is coming in the close future. Just very little things, like when the phone will ring, or when the post will come. It's a sense of 'knowing' that I never had before. I'm sure it's linked and so I've been trying to flex this 'intuitive' muscle as I've come to call it. Before I look at the tie, I know it will be bottle green.

"So, what do you think?" I do an over the top twirl once the tie is fastened into place, and watch Barkley descend into a fit of giggles at my gesture.

"Breathtakingly beautiful mate," he says and I can't help but laugh along with him. The salesgirl rolls her eyes and walks away, leaving me to get changed back into my normal clothes. It's at this moment that I think how strange it is that the suit feels like just as much of a costume as my iLUMiNO get-up.

As Barkley and I climb into the train carriage home, pushing our way past push-chairs and loitering teens to find two seats near one another, I feel a strange sensation running through me. My guts feel unsteady, like butterflies are crawling within me. Something is wrong but I don't know what. I look around and don't see anything out of the ordinary. Then I feel a pull and I am not on the train anymore. I am back in the Neutral Zone. Time is standing still. Before me is Metatron. The ethereal, beautiful, blue and purple-eyed being. Purple robes swathed his body, billowing behind him.

"Where are we?" I asked looking around.

"Where do you think we are?" Metatron asked cryptically, tilting his head to one side like a confused puppy.

I looked harder, focusing on my surroundings. The world around me became populated. Train seats. The train tube. Stationary. No, not stationary, but sideways. Carnage surrounded me, people strewn around the cabin. I couldn't tell if they were dead or alive.

"What is happening?" I asked of the robed-being, confusion overflowing me in waves.

"You had a feeling that something bad was going to happen..." the answer came.

"Wait, this is what the bad feeling is about?"

The response came in the form of a single nod.

"But what happened?"

"Think, Aaron, you know what happened or what is about to happen. You know how to stop it too."

I emptied my mind, trying to ignore the world around me. I breathed in. Out. In. Out. I looked inside myself for the answer and found it almost instantly. The tunnel up ahead had collapsed and we were heading towards it at full speed. I had to do something to stop it.

"Well done, Aaron," Metatron said as the Neutral Zone disappeared around me and I found myself back in the train compartment.

"I have to go to the loo," I said, pushing up from my seat and walking down the aisle, not waiting for Barkley to respond.

I knew what I had to do. I knew what was going to happen if I didn't intervene. I couldn't let innocent people die. As I strode up the centre of the train towards the front compartment, and the toilets, I felt the machine pulsing underneath my feet. Shutting myself in the coffin-like bathroom, I could feel the energy flowing through its steel body. Exhaling, I reached with my mind, connecting with the wheels and cogs. I allowed my awareness to spread out, through the electrics, the components of the train, and to the engine. Bingo. Just what I wanted. Pushing the power from my mind, not my brain but my mind, and with all my might, I willed the engine to stop. I had connected the life force of the mechanism of the engine. The spluttering could be heard from all over the compartment, people looked around and grumbled between themselves, knowing something had gone wrong with the mechanics of the train. As far as they were aware, the train had broken down.

The train continued to coast, not slowing down fast enough to come to a standstill before we reached the collapsed tunnel. I pushed my awareness outwards, my mind grasping hold of the brakes and engaging them at once. Within a matter of seconds, the train came to an abrupt stop. Bracing myself against the toilet wall, I allowed myself to exhale properly for the first time. I had done it. iLUMiNO had done it. I sat down on the toilet, the golden aura that surrounded my body was dissipating I was still dressed in the iLUMiNO garb that had appeared on my body when the bathroom door had closed. It was a strange feeling that I had, knowing I could manipulate things with my mind, like the gun, not just little things, but huge roaring machines full of fuel and pistons. I had stopped them, with my powers. For the first time since becoming iLUMiNO, I was aware, I felt that we had become one and the same. I would embrace him and I was more open to finding more and more skills I might be able to use as iLUMiNO. I said a silent prayer of thanks to Metatron for guiding me through the situation, knowing that I could call on his support when needed, as I navigated the new world I had been thrust into. It afforded me the space to breathe.

Collecting myself as I washed my hands, I saw in my reflection my face returning to my own and my costume dematerialising as my normal clothing reappeared. Opening the toilet door to the train carriage and walking back to Barkley, feigning surprise as I asked him, "What the hell was that?"

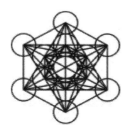

THE RED CARPET ISN'T at all what you'd expect it to be. For starters, it's about ten feet long and leads to nowhere. You have to step across the pavement and into the cinema, leaving the red carpet behind you. Lining the carpet are about a hundred people with cameras. Huge flashes going off constantly. You hear a chorus of, "Who is that?" when the lesser cast members make their way into the golden doors of the Empire building, the extravagant cinema in Leicester Square, London lit up in all its glory with its fine, palazzo-style exterior, reminiscent of its architectural and historic significance.

Surprisingly, there's no chorus of confusion when Barkley and Darcey shimmy their way from photographer to photographer. Both of them have become an overnight sensation and are more recognisable together than apart. I walk a few feet behind them, allowing Barkley to hog the limelight. After all, it is thanks to him that I'm here. As I focus on not falling on my face in front of the audience, I do a bit of celebrity spotting. Keanu Reeves isn't anywhere in sight yet, but there are a couple of actors from Coronation Street that I recognise and a few TV personalities, which is just as exciting for a premiere-virgin like me.

Once I'm ensconced in my seat, I feel immediately relaxed. All the nerves I'd felt before walking the red carpet had gone and I thought I can relax and watch the film. Just as the title screen appears, Keanu Reeves crosses the front of the cinema, taking his seat front and centre to a raucous round of applause. I join in, my heart skipping a beat, it feels strange that we can tie so many emotions to a person we have never met before. About half-way through an immense fight-scene, I get an urge to leave the cinema. Too strong to ignore. It feels like somebody is grabbing hold of the life-force within me and pulling me. I can't resist.

Apologising to the unfortunate people sharing my row, I edge my way out of the cinema, knowing that Barkley will presume I need to visit the toilet again. My legs carry me through the foyer and towards a door labelled, 'staff only'. Ignoring the sign, I try to push and pull the door but find it locked. I find myself looking around to see if anyone is watching, checking the ceiling and walls for cameras. No one is around, and the only cameras I spot are facing the box office and the main entrance. I place my hand on the door, a golden glow encompasses it as it goes halfway through. Quickly leaning my head on the door, I push it through making sure there is no one on the other side. Seeing the corridor is empty, I continue to walk through the door. As I did, I realise I've taken on the form of iLUMiNO. I find myself walking down a long, grey corridor that reminds me of the hospital I spend a lot of my time in. It is eerily quiet. No noise except for an intermittent buzzing. I stop myself. Trying to tap into that intuitive part of me that can sense what is wrong. I cast my mind back to Metatron and his advice. I need to breathe and focus. My mind's eye spreads out around me. I picture it like tendrils of golden light seeping out of my body, searching to find out what has set me on edge. The feeling is reminiscent of that on the train and so I know I need to act quickly. There's something very sinister occurring around me. I take a deep breath. Catching my reflection in a glass doorway, my golden glow adding light to the dimly lit corridor. I am iLUMiNO and that is all the ammunition I need. My intuition reaches out and grabs ahold of something I'm not familiar with. But I can feel the evil coming from within it, imprinted onto its cuboid body. Ticking like a clock. Before I can command my feet to move, my brain commands my body to dissipate and appear next to the source of the sound. The source of that bitter energy. My awareness tells me that I am below the screen showing the film I'm supposed to be enjoying. I can hear the car crashes and screams above, emanating from the big screen. My eyes find the source of my discomfort. A box is taped to a beam and a red wire and a blue wire stick out from beneath an old mobile phone.

A bomb.

"Shit," I whisper to myself as I look at the foreign object before me. What the hell do you do with a bomb? How do you stop it? I reach my mind into the machine, feeling for the way it works, how the components fit together. The realisation hits me like a brick. There's less than a minute before the bomb will go off. Forty seconds to be precise. The ticking noise fills my brain as I push my mind further and further into the depths of the bomb. *How do I stop it? What the hell do I do?* I begin to panic, my breathing quickens. That's when I hear a familiar voice. *Slow down, Aaron. Breathe in. Breathe Out. What does your mind tell you to do?*

"It tells me to get this bomb as far away from these people as possible."

I grab the bomb in both hands, doing the only thing I can do. I fly up through the dimly lit ceiling underneath the cinema. Flying up through and into the auditorium, I do not know if the people watching the movie saw me, I don't have time to stop and think. Flying straight through the roof and attic space of the theatre and out into the open night. Flying as high as I can, my breath begins to freeze the higher I get. Below me, I can see the theatre and a quieter Leicester Square; the streets are empty. I thank God that the cameras have all vanished, or have they? I'm approximately two kilometres up in the air above,

Loindon with a bomb in my hand. I stop flying and assess my situation. *Breathe Aaron.* My awareness tells me to throw the bomb into the air and get away from it before it explodes. There are ten seconds left on the clock and I stare at it, I just stare at it in my hands, my breath hitting the timer as it counts down. As soon as it gets to three seconds, I throw the device up into the air above my head and watch. That is the point when I should have begun the descent, but instead, I watch in awe as the bomb explodes at first in silence. And then a bright flash of gold, white light. And then comes the deafening boom. It is beyond anything I could have ever imagined. It looks exactly like something out of a movie.

I am thrown backwards. The noise and shock waves that hit me are intense. I hear glass shattering underneath me as I begin to fall. I can hear people screaming and running out of buildings, alarms ringing out. I'm falling out of the air, but I am concussed, I can't focus, I'm freezing and I'm falling, the only thing that's warm is my neck. Holding onto my neck I realise a foreign object protruding from it. My hand reaches up and I feel blood. Hot and sticky. Thick. Dripping over my hand. A blinding pain screams around my body. I look at my fingers and they are covered in blood. As I breathe, as I fall, I am certain that I have done enough to keep the people safe.

Thoughts fall back into my head and I realise how vulnerable I am. It's like being killed off in your first ten minutes of playing a new computer game. I have all these abilities... and I'm going to die...

EIGHTEEN
From Hero to Villain

In and out of consciousness on the twenty-second free-falling descent, I managed to flip over and saw the red carpet on the ground coming up to me so fast that I braced for impact by crossing my arms across my head and face. The orange glow that emanated from my body exploded creating an energy force that knocked some bystanders over, it cushioned my impact. I slowly stood up and turned, to a frenzy of flashing cameras and reporters shouting out my name.

"You're bleeding!" they shouted.

"iLUMiNO!" they shouted.

A small piece of metal was stuck in my left carotid artery. My body was trying to push it out as the foreign object that it was, and I could feel it slowly emerging. I gave it a hand and pulled the shiny metal shard out, placing my hand on the wound; blood spurted out and a photographer fainted.

My wound healed fairly quickly; the blood still evident on my costume.

"What happened?" a reporter shouted out. "Are you ok?"

I was just about to answer when Darcey Dyson approached taking the piece of shiny metal from my hand and placing it in a clear bag.

"I'll tell you what happened, our dear friend iLUMiNO has got a lot of explaining to do. Creating an explosion to boost one's persona, is quite frankly terrorism, and for that, he should be arrested right now."

The frenzy of the cameras started flashing again, and the crowd of reporters and fans were all shouting at me.

I didn't know what to say. I was shocked, horrified that people would think badly of me. I could see what everyone else could see. Me, iLUMiNO, bleeding in public, near the site of a bomb. It was a media frenzy. I needed to leave, now.

People began to pour out of the doors of the cinema like a tidal wave sweeping a sandy beach, I pushed against the grain. Pain thumped inside my head. I knew that in all likelihood I had a concussion. You pick these things up when you work as a porter. I had to get back in side, Barkley would be looking for me. I imagined the inside of the auditorium, and in creating the golden portal, I stepped into it and instantly everyone disappeared along with the noise. Inside the theatre was relatively quiet and the last few people were leaving the building, the film was still playing on the big screen. I looked around sheepishly as I slowly morphed back into myself. Rubbing my head, I had what felt like the worst hangover ever. I started to make my way outside like everyone else, but before I did, I was tapped on the shoulder.

I turned around and it was Barkley.

"Looking for me," he asked.

I looked at him, he looked at me. He knew.

I looked down at the floor. My heart sank. My friend knew that I was a liar.

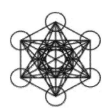

BOMB GONE WRONG, AND similar headlines, were now covering the front cover of every single newspaper. As was the main story on every single news station. A picture of me. Well, of iLUMiNO, standing atop the red carpet outside the premiere in London with a piece of the bomb in my hands covered in blood. When the news reporters compiled all the available footage, you saw iLUMiNO flying in the air above the city then reappearing seconds later as a bomb blast shakes the whole city. The footage was damning. The headlines all relayed the same information. WANTED: iLUMiNO. All because Darcey switched the angle of the story. She was milking all of the attention, of course. Barkley was shellshocked by the whole thing. He closed all communication with me. I didn't know if he hurt because I lied to him, or he believed the lie that Darcey had implied to the world. I was dying to tell him that it was all a big mistake. That I was the hero and that I saved them all. But that felt like an impossibility right now. We were all living in the aftermath of the bombing, many of the patrons of the cinema including Keanu Reeves were having a crisis of faith after their brush with death. Little did they know that they would have died, had the 'most wanted' criminal not intervened.

I read the words in horror. Each word sent a shockwave down my spine, the headline dominating the page.

FROM HERO TO VILLAIN. Towards the capture of the world's most hated creature. I read on.

What happens when a hero turns villain in front of your very eyes? Well, exactly what is happening to iLUMiNO. The creature once hailed as a hero has fallen beyond all repair after a bomb blast in the City of London. Damning evidence shows iLUMiNO holding the weapon of mass destruction above the celebrity-filled cinema, before vanishing into thin air in an action that sends chills through every person who watches the video. The questions grow and grow.

What caused our hero to fall from grace? What message is he trying to send? Did he have a change of heart? Or did the plot go wrong?

Our reporter spoke to Darcey Dyson, the famed news anchor who has had run-ins with iLUMiNO in the past. *"I am frankly terrified and astonished by the actions of iLUMiNO to tell you the truth. He saved my life, and the lives of others, but now he is trying to take them. This detrimental development puts us all at risk until he is captured and brought to justice. If you're reading this iLUMiNO, do the right thing and come forwards. Don't put anybody else at risk from your volatile actions."*

That's quite a change of tune from Dyson but nobody knows iLUMiNO better than she does. Originally leading the mission to track down and identify a hero, she has now placed herself at the head of the charge to find the UK's most wanted criminal.

They thought that I was guilty. They think that I tried to kill people, or at the very least that I was trying to make a statement. I wished I could tell them the truth but who is going to listen to me, the most hated person in Britain. The social media tirade was worse. I wanted to crawl into a hole and never come back out. God knows what I would do if they found out it was me. There was a constant barrage of faceless people calling for my incarceration at the very least, or my execution at the very worst. The current social media spin on the story was that iLUMiNO had placed the bomb intentionally outside of the cinema in order to 'fake' save the masses and hail himself a hero, but that something had gone wrong in the process and he'd either got cold feet or programmed the bomb wrong, leading to it self-destructing mid-air. And, to be honest, the videos did appear to prove this. Without a shadow of a doubt.

Aside from the hatred I was facing, I was concerned about the fact that somebody had placed that bomb and they'd gotten away with it. Out there, free as a bird, was a person who had tried their damndest to kill a cinema full of people. And, they would have been successful too. Switching out my coffee for a large gin and tonic, I stared out of the window trying to figure out my next move. I could call in an anonymous tip to the police that iLUMiNO didn't cause the explosion, but who was going to believe that? Plus, they'd trace the call back to me, I was certain. I could hunt down the bomber myself, but I had no idea where to start. Or I could trust that the police conducting the investigation would be unbiased and not just pin this on me. Not knowing what to do, I signed up for extra shifts at work, hoping that as my mind was occupied, I might have a light bulb moment and come-up with some crazy-good idea that was going to save me and bring the actual perpetrator to justice.

As it turned out, the hospital wasn't the best place to get away from the situation. Our fallen hero was the talk of the town. Both patients and staff did nothing but talk about it. iLUMiNO had replaced the weather as the most covered topic. I managed to meet Leigh for lunch during one shift out of five. It tended to work that way, only when our schedules worked out. Sitting at our usual spot, sipping luke-warm coffee, she chattered away like she always did. I wasn't really listening and she noticed, almost straight away. I say almost because Leigh could talk to a brick wall if she wanted to.

"So, what do you think of this iLUMiNO thing?" Her words broke me out of my stupor.

"What do you mean?" I answered, aware that I sounded stupid.

"You know. Do you think they'll catch him?" Leigh's face contorted with concern. She absentmindedly rubbed her growing stomach. I could tell that she was worried about bringing a baby into the world. Many people, both online and in-person, were talking about what it would mean for an actual real-life supervillain to be on the loose. I did my best to remind them that he'd not been found guilty yet, but couldn't get too defensive or I'd be sussed out.

"Do we know for certain that he did it? It seems out of character for him, doesn't it?" I asked, feigning ignorance.

"I mean, the video is pretty bloody clear! Don't you think? The guy has shards of the bomb in his hands."

"There could be another reason for that," I hedged.

"And what might that be?" Leigh laughed at my poor attempt to remain impartial.

"That he found the bomb and was trying to save people?"

"You sound like Barkley! He's been saying the same thing since it happened. It's like he doesn't want to believe that the guy that saved him has turned bad. When he definitely has!"

"Barkley said that to you? Those were Barkley's actual words?" Leigh nodded her head at mine. "You know what's funny..." Leigh carried on. "I was certain that you were iLUMiNO for a while!"

I was being bated. Leigh was digging for information in her usual way. She wanted me to fess up for myself and was giving me the opportunity to do that. I think she knew the possibility of me actually being iLUMiNO was far beyond crazy, and that would keep me safe for now. I needed to keep my identity from Leigh for a little while longer or until I'd figured this out. Maybe there would be a point in the future where I could tell Leigh who I was but now wasn't the time. Maybe when things got back to 'normal', if they ever did, me and Barkley can recover from this. I didn't tell Leigh that Barkley had stopped talking to me. I vowed to myself at that exact moment that I would tell them both everything. Once my name was cleared. But not now. Definitely not now.

NINETEEN
Growing Up

I felt like I didn't belong anymore. I'd not picked up any agency shifts at work for over a week. I'd turned my phone off and all I seemed to do was eat, sleep, watch car crash television and repeat. No one had heard from me in a whole nine days, and I hadn't heard from anyone else either. I would order take out most evenings and continue to eat junk food throughout the day if I was awake.

I took to the bathroom to brush my teeth, as I'd not brushed them in days. Looking in the mirror, I smoothed over my newly grown beard with my hand; my hair was a mess and I'd got dark circles surrounding my eyes. I looked rough. I felt rough. I was depressed.

It had been a while since I had felt like this. Years, in fact. I recognised the symptoms of depression, but I didn't even care about trying to do anything about them.

When my parents died, I'd hit rock bottom, and if it wasn't for my friends getting me the right treatments and being there for me, getting my medication, making sure I was taking it, taking me to my therapy appointments and just being there for me, I don't think I could have done it, they were amazing.

Where were they now I asked myself as I flicked on the television, sitting just in my underwear and a fleece blanket draped over my shoulders. It was 5 pm and I had just woken up. I opened the pizza box from the night before and ate two slices of cold dry pizza while flicking through the channels. Opened bottles of Budweiser were dotted around the sideboard with the photo frames of Mum and Dad. I grabbed at them one by one. The third bottle had some remnants in it. I took a swig and used it to swallow the dry pizza.

Outside through the window, I could see old Mr Williams struggling with his wheelie bin. I normally bring it up the drive for him, from his back garden. His front garden has some steep steps in it, I could see he was really struggling, but I didn't even feel guilty sitting there watching him.

Most TV channels were still talking or referencing iLUMiNO. I just kept on changing the channels until something none related came on.

I threw myself back in my chair, rubbed my hands through my hair, and I could feel tears beginning to pool in the corner of both eyes.

I just wanted this horrendous situation to work its way out, once I could prove I was innocent as iLUMiNO, then I could concentrate on my friendship with Barkley. These were my priority thoughts, but I wasn't getting anywhere.

I wiped my tears and continued to watch Mr Williams struggle.

"Take me to a safe place," I said to myself. Then I cried out, louder and angrier, "Metatron, take me to a safe place!"

The room faded, disappearing like the pixels of a computer screen going out one by one. Each light became white. I was sitting in my same armchair, still in my underpants with the fleece blanket wrapped around my shoulders.

I was in the neutral zone.

"Metatron?" No reply.

"Metatron!" I shouted.

Nothing.

I stood up from the armchair and suddenly I was in my bedroom when I was a kid.

A Keanu Reeves movie poster called Chain Reaction adorned the wall. It was peeling off on one corner. I slowly pressed it back into place as I was trying to work out what was happening.

"What's going on?" I said to myself.

My bedroom was directly above the kitchen, and our floorboards were so thin I could sometimes listen to every word spoken in the kitchen below. I could hear my mum in the kitchen downstairs singing along to the radio. I imagined her swinging her hips and dancing along to the tracks as she went about her morning. The sweet smell of bread wafted in under my bedroom door; she was baking again. Walking across to the bathroom, I could hear my dad, from the direction of his voice I could tell he was probably sitting at the kitchen table. He was chuntering to himself. The newspaper's rustle was loud. I could hear him shuffling the paper upstairs as he said the words Tony Blair followed by some expletives. Mum's reaction was typical of her.

"We'll have less of that language at my kitchen table," she said, followed by the next verse of the song she was singing.

The calendar on the wall in the upstairs hallway showed it was Thursday the 31st of July 1997. I was twenty one today.

But I was more concerned about what was happening.

"Metatron," I whispered. "What's happening? Where am I?"

"You're in the Neutral Zone. You know where you are," came the mesmerising familiar voice. "Time as you know it has stood still, but while you are in here, you can work things out, get to the bottom of things. You know this already, that's why you are here."

"I'm home" I said. This is the day my parents die, I don't want to relive that day ever again."

"Then don't. You don't have to do anything you don't want to. But your mind, your consciousness, brought you back to this moment. Maybe there is something to take away from it. Observe it as it happened, like an invisible fly on the wall watching the pre-recorded scenes unfold, or relive it as it happened, embody your entire existence as a twenty one year old."

I looked at the calendar again, and with a crack in my voice I said, "I'm going down to see mum and dad again." Metatron smiled at me before he faded away. I looked in the mirror and I was young again. I was wearing an Independence Day t-shirt from the movie. I used to wear this t-shirt to sleep in since it had gotten bleach down one side. I pulled it up closer, it had the same bleach splash marks.

"Aaron," Mum shouted upstairs. "Are you coming down, Birthday Boy?"

"Coming Mum", I said. My eyes filled up with tears of love. I wiped them from my face and descended downstairs.

I entered the kitchen and stepped up to Mum behind the sink. I put my arms around her, placing my head on her shoulder, and we slowly rocked to the rhythm from the radio.

"I love you Mum," I said.

"Someone's woke up a different person that's for sure," Dad said as he lowered his paper.

"I love you too Dad," I said.

"Are you looking forward to your birthday BBQ?" Mum said wiping down a mug with a tea towel.

"I bet he's more looking forward to going to York for the weekend? Aren't you, my son?" Dad smiled.

The hug and love that I felt from my parents enveloped me like bubbles on top of water, there was no getting away from it. It was bliss. I let the scenes run their course. I knew that I was still Aaron Abbey, 43. I knew that I was still sitting in my living room in 2021 in boxers and a fleece, but this scene was magical. I just embraced it and went with the flow.

When Dad said, "I bet he's more looking forward to York," the scene changed. It was a week earlier and I was on the phone to Lottie.

My friends had arranged an overnight trip to the city that weekend.

Lottie was good at arranging things like this; she was like a project manager, booking our hotel rooms, taking deposits, arranging free drinks at various clubs and no doubt some surprises along the way. She would keep me up to date most evenings on the house telephone. So far there was me, Lottie, Leigh, Barkley, Penelope and Brenda who had decided that York was the place to be on the weekend of my 21st. She would be on the phone nearly every night, and Dad would go mad asking who was paying for the call. It wasn't until the week before, during a phone call to Lottie discussing York and the various pubs and clubs we were to visit, when mum took the phone out of my hand and said to Lottie. "Why don't you all get together next Thursday on Aaron's Birthday. You can all discuss it together then, can't you?" She handed the phone back to me and smiled.

Lottie was more excited than me. "Ooh, that's great. I'll let the others know!" she said her voice an octave higher. "What time? Ask your mum what time."

Mum answered back before I could even ask her.

"12 pm."

"Twelve o'clock," I said.

"Great, see you then," she was just about to hang up, then I heard. "Aaron, Aaron are you still there?

"Yeah, I'm still on the line."

"Do I need to bring anything?"

Placing the phone on my shoulder, I turned around "Mum, does Lottie need to bring anything? Food? Drink?" I asked, assuming this is what Lottie meant.

"No love, me and your dad will sort it. We'll get the BBQ out, won't we?" she said, looking at my dad, making decisions on his behalf. He nodded.

Putting the phone earpiece back to my ear, "No, you're good Lottie, just bring a big fat present for the birthday boy, that shall suffice."

We both laughed, "Great, bye." I could hear the tinkle of the bell on her phone as she slammed it down before it went to the dialling tone.

I stood there and thought about how young her voice sounded.

I phoned Barkley to ask him what he was going to wear. "Jeans and a t-shirt," he said.

"Shoes or trainers," I asked.

"Shoes, in case, were not allowed in a club with trainers on."

"Oh yeah," I said. "Do you fancy meeting me in town? I want to get a new outfit for York, and I'll need some new shoes now come to think of it."

"Sure," he said. "Why not. I'm not buying anything though, I'm broke. Lottie has cleaned me out, hotel money for York and your birthday present. I've got enough for York though, so don't let me buy anything."

The colours of the room swirled and faded; and I was back in my bedroom on the morning of my birthday.

I'd bought a new pair of Levi's jeans, loose fit, and an oversized white long-sleeved shirt with vertical stripes in blue, green, brown, and red. I was to wear this open with a white crew-neck t-shirt underneath.

Mum must have heard the water running in the bathroom as I brushed my teeth. The kitchen tap would bang when the pressure was released if someone used the sink in the upstairs bathroom. Dad had been going to fix it for years, but never got round to it.

"Aaron," she shouted upstairs. "Would you like a cooked breakfast?"

"No thanks, Mum. I'll just grab some toast, if we're having a BBQ later. I don't want to over-face myself," I said as I threw on my dressing gown.

It was really weird being inside my own body saying things that I know I said all those years ago.

I rushed downstairs to find a pile of cards and some presents on the kitchen table. Dad always wrote my birthday cards; sometimes, he'd write a funny verse inside. There was a biro and some writing paper with doodles and scribbles on the table next to his folded newspaper. It was evident that he had just written on my card. He sat there with his arms folded.

"Come on then," he said, open your cards.

Mum placed a cup of coffee down and a slice of toast with jam, no butter, cut into triangles in front of me, just how I liked it.

Dad tapped a blue envelope with the biro from the table as Mum turned around to watch as I opened it. The front of the card read 'Happy 21st Birthday Son' in gold embossed italic writing.

On the inside in bold black print, it read 'Happy 21st Birthday - Have a great day!'

Underneath Dad had written a verse, I was expecting it to be funny, and borderline rude, maybe some toilet humour as is usually the case, but it wasn't like that at all, not this time, it read...

Son, we are so proud of the man you are growing up to be.

You will always have our unconditional love.

Happy 21st Birthday to our beautiful son

Love from Mum & Dad.

"Deep for a Thursday morning," I said with a bit of a lump in my throat.

"It's true," Dad said.

I wanted to tell them that I had read Dad's poem about coming out. I wanted to tell them that I was from the future. I wanted to tell them not to go and collect my surprise birthday present.

I knew it wouldn't work. This wasn't real life anymore. It was a copy, like a recording. I was pulled from my thoughts.

"Now your present is not quite ready," Mum said, moving my plate to the side and wiping my toast crumbs from the table with a bleach-soaked dishcloth.

"Whatever it is, you shouldn't have," I said, licking the jam from my fingers.

"You won't be saying that when you get it," Dad said, screwing the used writing paper up into a ball and throwing it into the bin with a direct shot.

"Give us a smile birthday boy," and before I realised a flash had filled the room.

"Mum!" I moaned, "I'm still in my sleeps!"

"It's fine," she said, "You're only 21 once! Another photo for my album!"

It was 10 am, and my new outfit hung on the front of my wardrobe with the tags still in situ, my new black leather slip-on shoes still in their box. I contemplated wearing my new clothes for my little gathering in the garden this afternoon but decided against it.

Mum shouted upstairs to me, "Aaron we are just popping out, we will be thirty mins or so. Stay out of the garden, it's a surprise."

This was it; this was the last time I was ever going to see them alive. I shouted downstairs "No, don't go!" taking the staircase in three steps. I really wanted to stop them, but as I got to the bottom step, the scene carried on, I was back upstairs, and I shouted down, "Ok Mum, Dad, I will."

By eleven o'clock they hadn't returned. The younger version of me wasn't worried. But I was, it was like reliving your worst nightmare all over again. I came downstairs and I opened the other two cards and presents. One was from Uncle Perry, and the other was from Aunt Terri, I'd grown up knowing them as my Aunt and Uncle, but they were just close friends of my parents. I always took the mickey out of their names Terri and Perry, should be a double act, much to Mum and Dad's displeasure.

Aunt Perri had bought me a big silver key presented in a padded box with the number 21 cut out at one end. And Uncle Perry bought me a crystal pint pot with 21 engraved. I was putting it back in the gift box when the back door opened.

"Happy Birthday to you. Happy birthday to you. Happy birthday dear Aaron. Happy birthday to you!"

Leigh stood there and threw her arms open, gesturing a walk-in hug, I obliged. She hugged me so tight I could hardly breathe. She handed over a card and a white tupperware box, "Just a few nibbles for our gathering," she said.

"Let's go out into the garden. Dad's put the gazebo up; he's going to fire up the BBQ when they get back."

We sat in the shade, and it wasn't long before she had me in stitches. Knowing what she was about to tell me had the older me also in stitches.

She told me about how her new boyfriend walked in on her last night as she was getting changed into her nightie. She was fully naked when he walked in, and she didn't want him to see her fully naked, not just yet anyway, she said to save her embarrassment, she jumped onto the bed to get the duvet and cover her dignity. "The only thing is," she said in between laughs. "I jumped onto the bed so fast and so hard that I bounced back off the bed, up into the air, landing on the floor boobs and legs akimbo."

Tears of laughter streamed down our faces; both doubled over in hysterics.

"Pal," she said, "I wouldn't have minded, but I was in so much shock, my mouth was fixed wide open, imagine me laid on the floor, legs spragged apart like a turkey, I must have looked like a blow-up sex doll."

Barkley strolled into the garden with a bottle of wine and a card just as the laughter subsided.

"What have I missed?" he said plonking the wine on the patio table and taking his shades off.

Leigh gave me the look of death as if to say don't you dare repeat.

"Nothing," I said, "We were laughing at Leigh and her nighttime shenanigans with her new boyfriend." I gave her a cheeky grin, and we cackled even more.

"Oh, boy! I'll not delve any further; I'm too young and naive to hear talk like that." We all laughed as Barkley embraced me.

"Happy Birthday mate, I can't wait for York, we're going to have a great night mate."

"Is Lottie coming?" asked Leigh. "I still owe some money for the minibus."

"I'm here," she cooed as she pushed open the gate. "Where's the birthday boy?"

Penelope and Brenda soon followed it was so nice to have all my friends together.

"Where's your mum and dad?" Penelope said, rubbing the bright pink lipstick from her teeth.

The older me knew by now, and knew that there was nothing that could be done. I felt heartbroken again.

"They've have popped out; they said they'd only be thirty minutes, and that was nearly two hours ago," I said looking at my watch.

"There was a lot of traffic getting here," Brenda said. "Police cones and a diversion, the taxi driver said that there had been an accident."

"They are probably stuck in the traffic," Penelope added.

"Well, I hope they hurry up, "Lottie said. "I'm starving."

"I'll make a start on the BBQ," I said. "Barkley, can you give me a hand getting the food out?"

For just over an hour, I realised how happy I was surrounded by the people I love, the people around me who meant the most to me. We were making plans about Saturday night in York. I could hear a few whispers followed by giggles here and there. I was sure they were planning something, but it was good.

"I don't care what you're planning, so long as it's not a stripper. I will never forgive any of you if you book me a stripper."

Barkley teased, "Ahh mate, you will love her, I'm sure."

"Honest to god, I won't speak to any of you if you have booked a stripper!" They all laughed. It was a special moment, full of innocence.

The laughter stopped as two police officers walked into my back garden.

"Stop stop," I said. As the scene froze, the older me came out of the younger Aaron's body. The scene slowly faded away, the two policemen being the last figures to dissipate to white.

I was back in my own armchair in the neutral zone. Metatron came floating down in a purple and orange glow.

"Did you get what you needed?"

"I think so," I said. And, with that, the neutral zone disappeared as the living room faded back into view. The clock started ticking and I could see Mr Williams still struggling with his bin outside my front window.

I went straight outside, barefoot, in just my underwear, I didn't care. I walked across the lawn and got the bin to the end of the driveway for him ready for the refuse men to collect in the morning.

"My god, Aaron. You look rough! Put some clothes on or you'll catch a chill, either that or you may give some young woman a heart attack!"

He slowly pottered back down the side of the house and slammed his gate shut. "Thanks," he said peering over the top of the gate.

Back in the house, I turned on my phone. It lit up and beeped continuously for what seemsd like five minutes. 53 messages, 89 missed calls and 36 voice messages.

Selecting the green phone icon, I begin to create a group call: Barkley, Leigh, Brenda, Lottie and Penelope. Their names turned green as they connected to the call. I'm pleased that they all answered, even Barkley. I didn't give any of them a chance to say anything apart from hi, or hello... I cut straight to the chase.

"Guys, I need you over at my house asap. It's important."

I hung up.

TWENTY
The Truth

Leigh was the first one to arrive. I felt guilty the moment she burst through the front living room door. I should have realised not to scare or upset a pregnant woman like that.

"Aaron, Aaron," she said, "Thank god you're ok!" She squeezed what felt like the life out of me. "What's this all about? Are you ok? Hold on never mind. Tell me in a bit, I need ten pounds for the taxi. I came as quick as I could but I forgot my purse."

I handed her a ten-pound note and she ran back out to the taxi waiting at the top of the drive.

"Don't run!" I shouted up the drive to her, "Take it easy."

"Take it easy," she said on her way back, trying to catch her breath. "You've nearly given me a bloody heart attack. Now tell me, you are ok, aren't you? What's this all about? You got me worried. You look ok though, perhaps tired eyes, but you look ok," she said.

"I feel a lot better if I'm being honest."

After I'd hung up the group phone call earlier, I'd tidied myself up a bit. I'd trimmed my beard, had a quick shower, and tried to do something with my hair. I'd put some lounge clothes on and quickly tidied downstairs.

"Now come on tell me what's up?"

"I'll tell you when the others get here," I said.

"Is this something to do with coming out, because if it is, I'll kill you, we all bloody know anyway and no one gives a chuff so long as you're happy".

"It's nothing to do with that," I said laughing slightly. "But now you come to mention it, when the rest of the gang get here, I might as well tell them that I'm gay as well, you know while I'm at it. Have you spoken to anyone since I made the group call?" I asked sheepishly, wondering if anyone else was coming?

"Yes," she said as she took a cup out of the cupboard and switched on the kettle. "They are all coming".

"Even Barkley?" I asked tentatively.

"Yes, even Barkley, I know you guys have had a fallout, I'm not stupid you know."

"It wasn't like that," I said quietly.

"Well, whatever it was, now will be a good time to put it all behind you. Life's too short pal."

"Talking of short, have you got any shortbread biscuits? I'm craving them."

"I haven't. Sorry," I apologised.

"Digestives will have to do," she said sliding six out of the packet with one hand.

She took her cup of tea and digestive biscuits into the lounge and made herself comfortable using cushions to support her back. She rubbed her stomach and dunked a biscuit into her tea.

"So, do I get a preview of this or not, or are you waiting for the so-called gang?" She laughs.

Then her expression changed, her eyes widened and a smile greeted us both.

"Hey Bren, are you ok love?"

Brenda came through the front door; she still had her lanyard and name badge on from work.

"Hi Leigh, I'm ok thanks. I came as quick as I could. What's wrong, Aaron? I was in the middle of marking some school work. To be honest, I needed an excuse to break off, but not one like this. You got me worried. What's wrong? Are you ok?" She grabbed both my arms and stood me in front of her. She looked me up and down, "You look ok." She looked at Leigh and then back at me, "What's going on?"

"I'll tell you in a bit, when the others get here, I promise."

"Do you want a cuppa, love?" Leigh asked, taking over the kitchen.

"Please, black coffee, thanks." She asked Leigh "What's going on?" as they hovered over the kettle.

"I've told you, you will all find out as soon as we're all together, bear with me please," I said, anxiously wondering if I was doing the right thing.

We all sat down at the kitchen table, hot mugs in our hands, waiting. Lottie was next to arrive, and then Penelope. Lottie was mad at me stating she had to get the next-door neighbour to babysit, as it was an emergency.

"You're one lucky man," she shouted at me as if chastising a child, and pulling me in for a hug. "I wouldn't do this for anyone else you know. Now come on, what's up?" She glanced around and saw Leigh and Brenda sitting at the table. "Hi girls, are we all here?"

"I'm here," Penelope said as she entered the kitchen with her miniature poodle in one hand and a pink glitter handbag in the other.

"Is everything ok honey bun?" she said as she grabbed my chin pushing my cheeks together.

"Erm, I will be when I get everyone here. Can we go sit in the lounge?" I said.

We moved into the lounge while Leigh made hot drinks for Penelope and Lottie.

"Is he coming or what?" Lottie blurted out as she entered the living room with my superman cup in her hand. "Because if he's not, you might as well start and tell us what this is all about."

"He did say he was coming," Leigh confirmed.

"I'll give him a couple of minutes."

We all sat there, in silence. My best friends had all rallied round to my house at the drop of a hat, but the tension in the air was thick. Brenda was sitting forward nearly hanging off the edge of the sofa rocking slowly backwards and forwards. She held onto her cup so tightly you could see the whiteness of her knuckles. She was the brains of our group and she knew something wasn't right.

Leigh was dunking digestive biscuits into her drink while Lottie just sat there. Penelope was stroking her dog Sindee, we all waited. No one said a word.

The clock on the wall ticked and seemed to get louder. The tension was building, people had dropped everything and arrived so quickly, and to be sat in silence was making things worse.

Lottie broke the silence, "Look guys, I've left the girls at home with my neighbour, if nothing's going to happen, then I'm off, you can tell me about it later. Sorry Aaron, but I get anxious leaving them."

"They're okay," I reply. "Honestly they're ok. I promise."

"How can you promise something like that, don't be daft!" she said as she stood and put her hands on her hips headmistress style.

"I can honestly, I wouldn't lie to you. Now believe me when I say they are ok as we speak right now, I do, I promise you."

"You can't make promises like that Aaron, no one can," she said confidently.

"I can," I said.

She laughed nervously and began to gather her handbag and hat from the floor, "How?"

"Because he's iLUMiNO," Barkley said as he opened the front door.

TWENTY ONE
The Proof

After the laughter had died down, and Barkley had said hello to everyone, the room fell silent again and all eyes were fixed on me. Well, he didn't exactly say hello to me, he just gave me a nod and took the last remaining chair in the living room. He slouched back casually and looked around the room. He looked really well. He sat there and didn't look like a scorned friend that I thought he was. He looked happy to see me, and although no words were exchanged. I was happy to see him too.

"As if!" Leigh said stuffing another biscuit in her mouth. "I mean..." She laughed at herself with a mouth full of digestive biscuit on show, "I'll be honest, I did at one point think that you could be the infamous iLUMiNO, but then reality kicked in. I told you at work, didn't I?" She continued to laugh at herself. "This is going to be good. Oh, I'm glad I came now!" she said rearranging the cushions and getting comfortable.

Brenda looked directly into my eyes, as if she was piercing my soul. Bluntly and to the point, "Are you?" she asked.

Lottie shoved Brenda's shoulder as she laughed out loud. "Are you seriously asking him if he's iLUMiNO?" she continued to laugh, "Oh, don't make me laugh, I'll need to go to the toilet, weak bladder!" she laughed.

I could tell by her laugh that she was deflecting, it was a nervous laugh in case the answer was yes.

I had to tell them. I had to let them in on my secret, but most of all, I wanted to tell them that I was innocent and that I had not planted the bomb. That was the main reason behind this. I wanted my friends to believe me when I said it wasn't me. I wanted my friends to reassure me that everything was going to be ok, and that we would get through this, together. The only obstacle in doing this was that I had to reveal the biggest secret I have ever held.

"He's right," I said with my head held low. I felt ashamed admitting that I was the world's most wanted terrorist. "But I'm innocent," I said with passion lifting my head up so they could see my face. I was upset, I didn't want them to judge me.

Leigh didn't say anything as she struggled to get up from the chair, but when she did she put her arms around me and I placed my head on her shoulder, she always mothered me.

Lottie was in denial straight away, "Is this some kind of a wind-up? I haven't got time for this, really I haven't, I've told you my kids are with the neighbour and I'm freaking out. I'm off." She grabbed her bag and her coat and walked past me and Leigh, heading towards the front door.

"Lottie," I said. "They are ok. I promised you, didn't I? Look."

Letting go from Leigh's embrace I reached out with my right hand. The golden glow of energy was emitting from my hand like I was holding onto something that was on fire. I drew a circle in the air which opened a one-way viewing portal to Lottie's living room. The twins were visible, sat on the rug in front of the television playing a computer game and her littlest was sat at the dining table colouring in. A woman sat on the sofa reading a newspaper.

"You see? I told you they were ok."

Lottie dropped her handbag and her hat at the door and slowly walked up to the portal, she stood right in front and looked through inside the portal that revealed her living room. She stroked the golden smoky edges of the portal as if they were a newborn puppy. She was mesmerised and bewildered. Slowly, she took her mobile phone from her pocket and pressed the recent call button, watching the neighbour eagerly. The lady who was sat on Lottie's couch, reading Lottie's newspaper, picked up her phone and said hello.

Lottie stuttered her words, looking around at the others, "I'm just checking you're all ok?" she said.

"We're all good," the neighbour said down the phone. "Take your time. The girls are colouring and playing Xbox games. Is everything ok at your end?"

Lottie said, "Yeah, everything is fine." She hung up the phone.

Sitting back down on the sofa with the others, her face was still and motionless as if she'd had years of botox.

"I... I don't know what to say," Penelope said, looking as shocked and perplexed as everyone else in the room. "Is this some sort of wind-up? Are we being filmed? Is this one of those reality TV shows?"

"What just happened?" Brenda said. "Can someone please explain what just happened?"

"Barkley has already told you," I said. "I am iLUMiNO."

Just saying those words out loud, for the first time even to myself, felt good. It felt revitalising to actually say those words and let my friends in on the biggest secret of my life.

"So, you're not gay then?" Brenda said

"Hang on a minute," Leigh said. "What's that got to do with what we have just seen? Gay or not, I'm not being funny, but we have just witnessed a miracle right in front of our very eyes!"

"You're the intellectual one, Brenda. Have you not grasped what we have just seen?" Leigh said.

"Yes, I am. It's just that, my brain can't rationalise what I've just seen, I really thought we were coming here for you to come out to us," Brenda said as she began rocking on the edge of her seat again.

Barkley just sat there stroking his chin. He remained silent.

"Ok," I said. "Yes, I am gay, there I've said that too. Not that you didn't know. But I am also iLUMiNO and I didn't plant a bomb. I am not a criminal. I'm not a terrorist. I'm still me. You guys know me, I wouldn't hurt a fly."

"Have you got any vodka? I need a stiff drink," Lottie said as she stood up and made her way to the kitchen, her skin pale and shiny with perspiration, she was in shock.

"I knew it, I bloody knew it!" Leigh said holding a cushion in front of her. "Do something else," she said, wriggling into the chair. "Come on, show us some more!"

"Yeah, show us iLUMiNO if you are him," Penelope piped up, "I'm not yet convinced. I don't know what I saw just now but..."

She stopped mid-sentence as I transformed into my alter ego. The gold embers surrounded my body. My face changed into that of iLU-MiNO and the purple costume and cape looked so out of place in my living room with my friends looking at me.

"I... I don't believe it," Penelope finished.

Lottie came back from the kitchen with a glass of clear liquid I assumed was vodka, she stood and froze, and she stared at me for what seemed like an eternity. I could feel her fear, the internal drum of anguish, it was a fear of the unknown. Her hands began to shake and she crushed the top of the thin glass, causing a deep laceration through the palm of her hand. Blood ran down her arm and the colour faded from her face. Brenda let out a small scream. Penelope put her little dog down and quickly pulled off her pink silk neck scarf rushing towards Lottie. She placed it on her lacerated hand and sat her down before she fainted.

All eyes were upon me as I walked up to Lottie, she pulled away in fear until I said, "Lottie it's me, Aaron."

Penelope was still stemming the blood, and Lottie wouldn't let me come near her.

"Stay away," she said. "Stay away from me." She was shaking, the fear was real.

I slowly edged towards her, repeating, "It's me Lottie, Aaron, let me help you."

By now she was crying and shaking her head, blood was all over her dress as Penelope tried her best to stop the bleeding.

I stood there in front of her, looking directly into her eyes, as my real face, the face that she recognised, came through the golden aura. I was still in the iLUMiNO costume, but I was Aaron Abbey. "See," I said "It's me. You're ok, I promise. Let me look at that hand."

"Let him look at your hand," Barkley said, the first thing he had said in a while. "If you don't, it's an accident and emergency trip. You're talking six hours in A & E. Do you want to be away from your daughters that long?"

She shook her head. "No," she sobbed.

"I won't hurt you," I said. "I promise." Lottie slowly extended her torn hand out to me. Penelope removed the blood-soaked neck scarf and you could see it was a deep cut, fatty tissue and ligaments were visible.

Holding her hand in the cusp of both my hands, an orange, golden glow surrounded my hands as they healed the wound. It felt warm and electrifying, I could feel dark energy, the pain, leaving her body.

Once the healing of her hand was done, I held onto her a moment longer, and that's when I saw her deepest of fears. She was once nearly abducted by a man in a car as a child and she has lived with this fear all her life. She knew what I saw, she knew I felt what she felt, and she let me, like a patient talking to a psychologist. It was like she agreed to share that information with me. Without verbally asking, it was an unwritten communication like our souls were having a full-blown conversation, she agreed to let me help her. The anxiety that she had lived with all these years, the fear and anguish that had built up inside, the evil dark memories that had scarred her, were now being released.

I could see the darkness being pulled away from her head, as it travelled down her arm and into my hand. It clearly made an electrical spark as it burnt on exit.

She pulled her hand away slowly; we had connected on a level that we have never connected on before. She looked at her hand and remnants of blood were all that was left.

"Thank you," she said in a meaningful soft voice. She wasn't shaking anymore. She was at peace with herself for the first time in a very long time.

Looking over at the broken glass on the carpet, I imagined all the pieces being together again. An orange glow surrounded the broken glass and the pieces on the floor, they lifted up from the carpet. Extending out my hand as I imagined it being one whole piece again, it slowly became the original glass as it landed in the palm of my hand.

"I wouldn't want anyone else to hurt themselves," I said as I put the glass down on the bookshelf. The vodka remained on the carpet.

I looked over at all my friends, all of them sat with bewildered looks on their faces, even Barkley.

"I didn't plant the bomb guys. I didn't, you have to believe me."

I felt emotionally drained, my voice cracked and I fell to my knees. The superhero before them crying like a child who has just lost his parents.

"I need you guys to know, I am not the bad person here."

"No, you're not mate," Barkley said as he pulled me up from my knees. "Darcey Dyson is and we're going to help you prove it."

TWENTY TWO
Reconciliation

The girls left that evening taking my secret with them. I believed them all when they promised me that they wouldn't tell a living soul about tonight's revelations. I had a knowing that they were being honest with me. Trust is a big thing and I know I had it with these guys. I was relieved to know that they all believed I was innocent. That was good enough for me, knowing I had the trust of my friends. Barkley stayed over that night; he didn't want to leave me on my own. We had a lot of catching up to do. He wouldn't accept my apology, not because he was still angry with me, but because he said I did not need to apologise. He understood what I was going through, he said in hindsight he would have probably gone about it pretty much the same way as I did.

He had matured a lot over the last few months. If ever there was a moment I was proud of my best friend, this was one of them. Barkley pulled out a bottle of spiced rum from the inside of his jacket pocket and poured two glasses. Taking the ice from the freezer we headed outside and chilled in the back garden. He put his feet up on the rattan table and took a loving drink from his glass. Looking up, I saw Mr Williams drawing his back bedroom curtains and then the light went out in his room. The moon was high, and the stars filled the night like a diamond-encrusted black velvet blanket.

Before the girls had left, Barkley had explained that whilst Darcey was on the air doing a live news broadcast, he was waiting around backstage, waiting for Darcey to finish her nationwide broadcast. Darcey had called him over on his burner phone to come and review the footage obtained from the This Morning studio. She told him that she had got compelling footage that proved what he saw was real. That the photo frame he saw of my mum and dad had been caught on some security camera footage from the studio.

Barkley continued with his story. He was waiting around backstage of the news desk, while Darcey was presenting, and he could see that her office door was ajar.

He had spent a lot of time at the news studios of recently and had become a regular face around the set and offices. No one saw him enter her office, but if they did, they didn't do anything about it.

He told me how he wasn't looking for anything in particular, but just sat at her desk with no intention to be nosey, just looking around her office from her perspective. Her screen saver was active on her computer showing pictures of her with various awards, photoshoots and pictures of her sitting at various news desks. He said he wiggled the mouse to stop the images popping up because they were making him feel sick, and as he did, he realised her desktop was still active.

She'd been on air no less than four minutes and her log in was still active.

He explained how he knew he shouldn't, but couldn't help it. He started to browse around her onscreen desktop.

"I went to her browser and it opened to the home page darceydyson.com. Her new website had a picture of her holding up this journalism award or something. I clicked it off straight away."

Continuing on as I listened, completely enraptured, he told me how he was just about to leave the desk, and go and sit back outside behind the news set when he saw a folder on her desktop. It read 'ILUMI'. Intrigued, he clicked into it.

Inside were other folders named, This Morn, News, Sighting, Interviews, Footage, and then there was a folder that made alarm bells ring. Aaron Abbey.

He said he cautiously clicked into it and when he did, "Up came images of you Aaron, taken over weeks. There were video files, photos, sound clips, aerial shots of the quarry where we camp. Pictures from inside the hospital, all of you, taken from security cameras."

The last folder he saw gave him goosebumps, he said that he saw a folder code-named TERMINATE.

He said his mouth went dry as he clicked into it.

The folder opened, showing links to explosive sites, photos of previous bombings that had dominated the news in years gone by. There was an app inside this particular folder called Onion Messenger. He told us how he wasn't able to open it as it was password-protected, but researching it, he said the Onion Messenger was an encrypted anonymous messenger service found on the dark web.

At first, he said, he thought that this was a folder for researching and gathering evidence regarding the bomb that went off at the red-carpet event. Just before leaving the office, he right-clicked on the TERMINATE folder icon using the mouse. It told Barkley instantly what he feared. The date the folder was created was one month before the bombing.

"She was plotting against iLUMiNO. I knew you were iLUMiNO Aaron," he said. "But you wouldn't let me in."

"I'm sorry," I said. "I really am"

"Stop apologising," he said. "I have told you, it's fine, we are all in unprecedented territory."

I was relieved to know that the girls and Barkley knew I was innocent without this information. They believed in me, they believed in iLUMiNO, but just knowing this new piece of information for me was nothing more than amazing. Like I could breathe again after nearly being drowned. The girls took all this really rather well, it was information overload for all of them. Not only did I come out officially as gay to them, which never got a mention may I add, I also came out as my alter ego with breath-taking spectacular powers, and to top it all off, Darcey Dyson was out to ruin my life, with the potential of killing people in the process.

The drink that Barkley poured was needed. He always knew how to make me feel better.

Even if my world and the life that I lead was in the hands of some power-crazy mad woman. I felt comfort in the knowledge that my friends were still my friends, and that I had got their support, just like I always had.

"We need a plan," Barkley said as he poured himself another shot of spiced rum.

TWENTY THREE
In My Defence

We didn't come up with any plan for most of the night, we just sat and drank. He wanted to see some of my skills and abilities, but I told him I'd rather not demonstrate anything outside, especially in my own back garden with the risk of the neighbours overlooking. I was in enough trouble as iLUMiNO. I didn't need the added risk of my own life being ruined by performing some parlour tricks for Barkley. He agreed. It didn't take long for us to finish the spiced rum that he'd brought, it was only a small bottle.

"I really fancy another drink. Have you got anything in?" He said, pouring the last drop from the glass down his throat.

"I had a splash of vodka left, but Lottie made use of that dropping the glass and the vodka all over my carpet earlier."

"Well, you could always go and get some, you know, without actually leaving your seat."

I didn't need to say anything to him I just looked at him, like a parent about to tell a child off. "Come on," he said, "just grab a bottle from the shelf at the supermarket."

"Mate, I'm not going to steal anything, they will have security cameras, especially on the alcohol. Oh yeah!' I scoffed, "I can see the news headlines now. iLUMiNO Terrorist, Alcoholic, Thief."

"Ahh come on pal, I just want a couple more drinks with you. You owe me remember, and besides I can't drive now, I'm way over the limit."

"Mate," I said. "I'm not going to be emotionally persuaded or blackmailed or whatever you want to call it, not now not ever."

His face sunk in and his eyes drooped down at the outer edges, his body withdrew like a child having his hand slapped for being naughty.

Those big brown puppy dog eyes, I'm sure I'm not the only one he can work those eyes on. He pretty much always gets what he wants.

"Ok," I said. "But not because you owe me, it's because I want another drink as well."

He smiled, "Nice one."

"I'm not taking it from a shop though, I won't steal, I never have done, and I won't start now. Have you got any liquor in at yours?" I asked, looking at him face on, he knew where I was going with this.

"Yeah," he said rubbing his hands together excitedly. "Kim will be in bed by now, you know my kitchen, yeah? Well, I've got another bottle; left-hand side bottom cupboard."

"Right. Two secs," I said as I made my way inside. He was watching me through the glass patio doors. This was my way of killing two birds with one stone, showing him some iLUMiNO magic and getting the booze from his house.

I created a portal that gave me the travel window, just by imagining Barkley's kitchen. I stepped through as myself, no iLUMiNO get up. However, the golden glow surrounded my body lit up my kitchen, shining out onto the patio. I stepped through into Barkley's kitchen. I turned back, and I could see Barkley sitting on the rattan furniture in my back garden. It did look really bizarre if I am honest, but I was getting used to it. I grabbed the bottle from the cupboard, but as I was about to leave, I heard a voice that I recognised. It was a voice that I couldn't put a face to, but I was sure I recognised it. I was certain it wasn't Kim. The voice mentioned the name iLUMiNO, I could hear it crystal clear. It was coming from Barkley's living room. I sneakily walked down the small hallway, leaving the portal open to my house. I peered into Barkley's living room and Kim was sitting on the couch with her back towards me watching the latest news broadcast.

The voice I could hear was coming from the TV. It was the girl that I saved from the attacker. I leaned onto the living room door and as I did it moved ever so slightly, but enough for it to make a creaking noise. Before Kim could turn round, I ran back to the portal. Barkley was there hanging his head through it taking in the view of his own kitchen from my house. "Wow," he said. "How cool is this!"

"Quick," I said. "Kim heard me."

He took a step back and I headed into the portal with his bottle of spiced rum in hand.

"Quick, grab me those marshmallows from the side will you?"

I rolled my eyes, grabbed them, and stepped back into my own house. The portal closed with a near silent woosh.

"Put the news on," I said. "There's a girl on the TV saying positive things about me. About iLUMiNO."

Barkley switched on my TV and flicked a couple of channels, and there she was. The young woman I had saved and staved off an attacker.

"He wouldn't do that, I know it in my heart. There is no way iLU-MiNO would plant a bomb. He scared off my attacker. I was about to be raped, I know I was. I wasn't strong enough to push the attacker off but iLUMiNO came and scared him off. If it wasn't for iLLUMiNO I don't know what frame of mind I would be in right now. I did sustain an injury that iLUMiNO healed just like he healed that famous guy, Barkley. But not only that, he actually asked my permission to do so. What kind of terrorist would do that? He asked my permission to be healed. Not only did he heal my open wound, but he also touched my forehead, looked into my eyes, and I looked deep into his soul and all I could see, all I could feel was love, and within seconds it was like a flash of energy something that I have never ever felt before. I felt every demon that I had, all the bad thoughts

and bad feelings I'd got, every last bit of negative energy that I had, disappear in an instant. It was like I had been hit with an electrical current that neutralised negative energy.

"Before all of this, before meeting iLUMiNO I was unemployed, I slept on my mother's couch, I needed alcohol to curb the pain of life, I was a nobody, and I was going nowhere in life. Whatever iLUMiNO did to me that night changed my life for the better. Because instantly I loved myself, instantly I accepted my flaws, instantly I knew what I needed to do to give my life a purpose. My life already had a purpose, don't get me wrong, but not a happy one. He helped me see the goodness in myself. iLUMiNO is no terrorist. He's an enigmatic being of love and compassion and balance."

The camera panned back to the reporter, not Darcey Dyson.

"iLUMiNO is still wanted for questioning over the attempted Leicester Square Cinema bombing. The investigation..."

I turned it off before the reporter finished his sentence.

"She's right," I said to Barkley. "When I am close to people, I can see a dark energy. It's like a life force all on its own. I know it's a negative energy, or some kind of darkness within a person, and I can pull on it, I can pull it out. I can alleviate a person's struggles in life."

"Did you do that when you healed me?" Barkley asked looking very serious.

"No, I didn't see any negative energy in you mate. I saw pain around your wound in the form of negative energy, that's what I did I pulled the negative energy out of your wound and it healed."

"Wow, mate. You could make millions just healing people! Imagine a world where no one dies, or has any pain. You could be the cure for cancer."

"Mate," I said. "I don't think you're thinking this through right. That would be a full-time job with no let-up ever. I like my life as Aaron Abbey, kind-hearted hospital porter, thank you very much. iLUMiNO isn't a permanent fixture in my life yet."

"Yet," he replied.

My phone rang, it was Lottie, I let it ring longer than I should, I just stared at the screen. Barkley saw that it was Lottie, "Aren't you going to get that?" he asked.

Picking the phone up, I switched it to speakerphone, "Hey Lottie, how are you feeling love? Barkley's still with me. You're on loud speaker, were having a good catch up, how are you?"

"I've just had the news on, and there was this woman, that you, that iLUMiNO, saved and she said he, you changed her life."

"We saw it too."

"Well," she paused. "That's what you did to me Aaron, you pulled every negative demon within me, out of me. My anxiety was through the roof before I came to yours today. You have made me feel like I am a new person, like all my worries and all my stresses, all the negative pressure I was under, has gone. Lifted as if... as if, I'm me again, like I have been reset."

"Wow," Barkley said. "You see Aaron, there's a market for this."

"I'm so pleased you're ok, and feel better, I didn't see your worries, your anxiety." I said, "I just saw it as a negative energy in you. That's the only way I can explain it."

"Well don't you see?" she said with a tint of excitement in her voice.

"See what?" I said.

"Aaron, you have got the perfect tool, weapon, or power, whatever you want to call it, you are the perfect person to show Darcey Dyson who she really is. You can save her from herself, and at the same time save yourself. Or iLUMiNO. Oh, you get what I mean, don't you? I don't get this two names thing. What I'm trying to say is. Pull the negative energy from Darcey. Do your thing! Maybe, just maybe she might come clean or do the right thing."

Barkley looked at me, raised his glass and said, "And now my friend, we have a plan..."

TWENTY FOUR
Fast Cars

I'd not celebrated my birthday in a long time, not properly at least, since my 21st. My birthdays all came and went, and I'd get cards and gifts from my close friends, namely the ones that were there when I got the devastating news about the death of my parents. So, it wasn't just a birthday, it was also an anniversary and I guess they felt part of that life experience that I experienced. The only card that I ever put up since my 21st was the card my mum and dad wrote all those years ago.

"Happy 21st Birthday Son," I read out aloud and stood it on the centre of my sideboard. Smiling to myself, I made it the centrepiece for another day like I had done every year since their deaths. The card was showing its age, but that's what made it more special for me. This year, I placed the poem that dad had written beside it. I needed to get a frame for that.

The doorbell rang. I was expecting Barkley, normally he would just walk straight in. It rang again, and then again.

"Ok, ok!" I shouted, making my way to the front door. I opened it to find Barkley standing there dressed in one of his finest suits with the biggest grin on his face; bottle of champagne and a card in his hands.

"Happy birthday, mate. What do you think to this ride pal? I thought we would arrive in style." He gestured out towards the road.

Sitting at the top of my drive was a silver sports car like no other. It was beautiful. I have never seen anything like it.

"Oh my god, Barkley!" I said. "You're kidding me! Is it a Ferrari?"

"It's a Bugatti Chiron, zero to sixty in 2.3 seconds. Mate. I'm buzzing. A three-million-pound car sitting on your drive."

"No way! Why would anyone pay that kind of money for a car?" I said walking around the exterior. "Why would anyone build one for that matter?" I ran my hand over the top of the gleaming metal. The curved structure and design made it look like something from the future, you could tell it was aerodynamically designed for speed.

"Three million quid," I said as I opened the driver side door. "How can you..."

He cut me off laughing, "I haven't bought it ya daft sod. I've hired it for the day. I've earned a fair bit of money since you..." he looked around cautiously in case someone overheard, "I mean iLUMiNO, came on the scene. So I've treated myself. Today," he said as he handed me a card and bottle of champagne, "we arrive for your birthday meal in style."

The smell of the interior was enticing. It felt like the car was hypnotising you to get inside, to feel the trim, the dashboard, to hold onto the wheel. I sat in the driver's seat. You could feel the luxurious quality seeping through, it made you feel important, sophisticated.

"We've got two hours to kill before your surprise birthday meal," Barkley laughed.

"Hold on," I said. "I'll just get my jacket."

Once upstairs I looked out of the front bedroom window, Barkley was standing in front of the three-million-pound Bugatti taking selfies. He was in his element. Anyone would have thought it was his birthday. The car had drawn a bit of attention and people were taking their time walking past it. Some kids on bikes were taking pictures, Barkley was loving it.

The jacket was fresh from the dry cleaners. Taking it out from the plastic covering, I put it on, straightened my tie and winked at myself in the mirror.

I was excited, I'd not felt like this in a long time. I knew what he was doing though. He was trying to take my mind off what was about to come.

Downstairs in the living room, I saw Barkley's birthday card on the side. I opened it, 'Happy Birthday Mate' it was signed BB. I stood it up next to my 21st Birthday card. Today was all about change. Hopefully for the better.

Locking the front door Mr Williams gave me a nod. He had come outside to see why a small group had gathered at the top of our drives.

"Nice wheels," he said. "Can you read my mind?"

"No," I laughed unsure what he was talking about.

"Has he committed the crime of the century or what?" Referring to Barkley.

"What do you mean?"

"Stealing that car! There's no way anyone in Redgrand could afford a car like that. He must have stolen it," he laughed.

Barkley was already in the driver's seat. I opened the passenger side door and slipped into heaven.

"Ready?"

"Ready!"

The engine roared into life. Revving the car, you could feel the power transcending the body of the vehicle. It felt good. He looked at me from the driver side and smiled. The smoothness of the car was unbelievable. You couldn't feel anything. It was like I was flying again. He would put his foot down for a couple of seconds, which would make my stomach feel upside down. We loved the attention. He drove through town. He was famous now and he loved people taking photographs of him driving this beast of human engineering.

We had the best two hours ever, driving through the countryside, owning it. He really was a true friend. He'd taken my mind off my birthday dinner but soon I recognised where we were, and the time was near on 6 pm.

He pulled up outside the restaurant and I felt my stomach turn again. Not because of the adrenaline. This time it was the nerves and anxiousness again.

We were about to change my life. One way or another, it was certainly about to change. But for better or for worse, we didn't know.

This time Barkley said in a more sombre tone.

"Are you ready?"

I nodded, "I'm ready." I was nervous, I was anxious. What if our plan didn't work?

Inside the restaurant it was all smiles, Penelope looked so elegant in her pink satin dress with the high neckline, blouson sleeves, and a thigh-high split added to its feminine charm. She looked lost without her lapdog like a ventriloquist without its dummy.

"Hello my darling," she said as she kissed me on the cheeks. "Happy birthday handsome!" she said pulling back to let Leigh in.

Leigh had outdone herself as well. She looked so beautiful, her hair pinned up with jewels dotted throughout it. Her dress was trimmed with colour co-ordinated decorative beads and sequins, plus beautiful diagonally draping layered ruffles which disguised her baby bump.

"Wow," I said. "Look at you!"

"Well, ya know, I thought I'd make an eff. Check out the wheels," she said. "Someone's been treating you!"

"Yeah, it was amazing. Bloody loved it. He's a good one," I said, referring to Barkley.

"Yeah, sometimes," Leigh said laughing.

Brenda came next and gave me a hug, "Here's my birthday boy!" She too looked so glamorous.

"No glasses?" I said.

"I've got my contacts in," she said. "I still can't see a thing though!" We both laughed.

Lottie waited until the gang had seen me. She walked up to me as graceful and elegant as a lady.

"Aaron," she said. "God, I love you. Thank you for you know. Just, thank you and happy birthday."

"You're welcome," I said.

I looked around and there was another couple sat at another table and a family of four on another.

"Is she not here yet?" I asked shifting my eyes around.

"Oh, she's here love. Double D is here."

TWENTY FIVE
Alternate Realities

We had arranged a meal for my Birthday, but there was to be a special guest, one who wouldn't be able to resist. Barkley came up with the idea saying that Kim couldn't make it, and he would invite Darcey as a plus one instead.

Darcey was now prime-time and wouldn't normally associate with us low-life, normal people. But the investigative journalistic demon inside her wanted more of Aaron Abbey. We knew she would jump at the chance to attend a birthday meal with Aaron Abbey and a few of his friends. And she did.

"She's confirmed," Barkley had rung me that morning. He didn't need to say any more, I knew who he meant. It was game on.

She swanned in from behind a lattice partition wall with fake ivy weaved in and out of it, which screened off the entrance to the toilets from the main eating area.

"Darling, darling," she said. Her dress was an egotistical overstatement for the little small-town restaurant that we were eating in. She looked like she was about to collect an award at the Oscars. Her bleached blonde short spiky hair and heavy eye makeup really did make her look like the James Bond villainess that I imagined she was.

"It's a pleasure to see you again, and on your birthday. Many happy returns sweetie," she came in to kiss my cheek, but with no physical contact. "Mwah," she said and then strolled over to Barkley.

Looking out of the window she said, "My my, someone's doing well for themselves. It's not a substitute for something else is it darling?" followed by a cheeky laugh. The girls laughed, along with her. I must admit, they were amazing. They were acting just as normal, no one would have guessed that the six of us had a plan in place.

A black car pulled up outside with blacked-out windows and parked behind the Bugatti. It stayed there for ages and no one got out of it. We all looked at each other, we were not expecting company. Barkley's face was pinched. I could see the thought pattern in his face. Was this the secret government people? If so, the plan definitely couldn't not go ahead.

"What's up with everyone," Darcey laughed, sat at the head of the table. "It's just my car waiting to pick me up."

The waiter came over and took our order. The meal was ok, nothing special, but ok. There wasn't anything unusual about the evening apart from the fact that no one brought up the subject of iLUMiNO, not even Darcey. I looked over at Barkley and I gave him an extended look, he knew what it meant.

"So, are you any closer with your investigation on the Leicester Square Bombing?" he asked Darcey outright. All eyes moved towards Darcey.

"Oh, I'm close," she replied. "Very close," she said, eyes transfixed on me as she took a drink from her wine glass.

"You are? That's great," I said. "So, you definitely think it was iLUMiNO that planted the bomb?" I asked making eye contact with her in return.

"I know for a fact it was ilUMiNO darling," she said. She leaned into the table and quietly said, "I've got proof."

She sat back and took another delicate sip from her glass. She owned the table right now, and she knew it.

"What proof?" Leigh blurted out knee jerk reaction style, then made shifty eyes at me as if to say sorry.

"What proof?" She laughed putting her glass down on the table. "Now if I told you that, I wouldn't be a good reporter, would I? And besides," she said rubbing her index finger around the top of her wine glass. "I wouldn't want iLUMiNO to trash the evidence, would I?" Again, she made direct eye contact with me.

"What if iLUMiNO was in this room? What if he was sitting at this table with you right now, what would you say?"

"I wouldn't be worried at all," she laughed. "I'd simply say 'Hello iLUMiNO!' I'm wearing a body mic, and I have a camera focused on me from my car, I don't have anything to be worried about."

"You're filming us?" Leigh blurted out again, this time with no apologetic glance over at me, slamming her coke down on the table. At the same time, Lottie sprayed her drink over the table.

Passing Lottie a napkin she said, "Darling, I'm filming me, don't worry. It's a dangerous job I do, you never know when you will need footage."

She had come with the hope that she would be able to get something from the meal. Bringing a micro-film crew, she was hoping that this meal would reveal more than meets the eye.

And boy was she right. The plan we had wasn't going to work, we all knew at this point it was game over. But not for me, that was it.

This was the moment. It was now or never, I felt an energy surge like no other. My cells ignited and I could feel the transformation taking place. I shifted into the neutral zone but this time I brought someone along with me.

Time froze and everyone stood still mid breath, the waiter began to pixelate to blackness, the restaurant followed, and eventually Barkley, Penelope, Leigh, Lottie and Brenda faded away. Leaving myself and Darcey sitting in the black room, sitting at an empty table with a light shining down on both of us.

I was iLUMiNO.

"I knew it," she said laughing and happy that her discovery was true. Looking around she stuttered, "How did you? What have you? Nevermind. I'm sorry Aaron, or ilUMiNO, the world has a right to know who you are and what you are capable of and now you have given me the biggest scoop I could ever wish for."

"Who I am?" I said standing up from the chair at the table.

"What I am capable of?" I said walking towards her.

"What I am capable of?" I said even louder.

"I will show you what I am capable of!" I waved my hands to create the construct of a scene.

Out of the darkness, in front of us as if the scene was on an actual stage, you could see me as myself outside the lifts at the hospital at work. The little girl Caroline sat in the oversized wheelchair, riddled with cancer. I showed her how I pulled the negative energy from her body. I was emotional as I watched it back, her little face unsure what was happening, but knowing that she was now going to be ok.

I swiped the scene across, and took us to a scene of Caroline playing in the school playground. Her hair had grown back. Ginger locks fell down her face and bounced around as she played with the other children.

Waving my hand again as if swiping a screen across, I showed her another scene.

I took Darcey to the attempted shoot out. Barkley laid on the floor blood pouring from his shoulder. The gunman with a gun towards Darcey's head.

"Do you remember what you felt at this moment?" I asked Darcey. "Do you remember the fear flowing through your body the moment you had a gun to your head?"

She remained silent.

"Do you?" I raised my voice.

"I don't ... I don't remember," she said, her voice cracking. I know she didn't want to remember.

"Let's remember," I said.

Darcey was no longer sitting at the table. She was in the same position as the reconstructed Darcey, her evening dress now even more out of place.

"Now do you remember?" I asked.

"Please," she cried, "I don't want to."

"Look at the gun, Darcey. This gun has just shot Barkley down and you are next. Is that what you want to happen?"

"No, no I don't!" she cried.

"Are you sure?" I said. "Because if I don't turn up, you're sure as dead. Shall we let that scenario play out?" I asked. She didn't answer.

I gestured with my hand three circles and the scene rewound to the part when Barkley entered the road and then it started to play out again. A recreation of what happened, the only difference was Darcey was still wearing the evening dress. Darcey was in the scene again. I stood watching from the side.

"Stay where you are," the gunman shouted at Barkley. "I only want one death today, don't make it two."

Darcey moved her eyes, just her eyes, as she looked at me in fear.

I shrugged my shoulders. "The world doesn't need me," I said, as I stood back and watched with my arms folded. "Barkley will survive the shoulder bullet; I don't know the extent of your injuries yet because we haven't got to that bit yet. You know what happens when iLUMiNO comes and changes your destiny. Let's see what happens when he doesn't come, shall we?"

I felt really bad letting this play out. Darcey was getting more and more upset and I didn't like toying with her emotions. But I had to carry on.

The gunman shot the gun into the air, the camera and sound man came into vision, albeit pixelated, they were not relevant to this current play out.

The gunman grabbed the real Darcy's hand and spun her around, pulling the back of her head onto his chest. The real Darcey screamed, "No not again! Please no!"

The gunman took the gun from the side of Darcey's head and pointed it directly at Barkley. "Stay back, or I will shoot," he said, flipping the weapon back and forth from Darcey's head to Barkley and back, just like he did at the real event.

"Put the gun down," Barkley said.

"This is what I originally said as iLUMiNO," I pointed out. "But without me appearing, it looks like this scene is now playing out very differently."

I was now just an observer. Darcey was a participant of a scene she was party to in real life, real-time to her, but this version would have totally different endings.

"Please don't do this," she said. I don't know if she was directing this at me or the gunman. Either way, I let the scene play out.

Again, the gunman said, "Stay where you are. I only want one death today, don't make it two."

"Put the gun down," Barkley said taking two steps closer.

Bang, the gun went off as he shot it into the air. Darcey screamed out loud and appeared to be more scared than she was when it happened the first time around.

"I said step back," the gunman repeated, even more agitated. This was new territory now.

Barkley took one step closer and BANG. The gunman shot at Barkley just like he did in the real event, Barkley took the bullet in his shoulder, falling to the ground instantly. He was out cold.

"All I can do is watch," I said.

Darcey was screaming and struggling to get out of the clutches of the gunman.

She looked helpless but I had to let this play through.

She managed to free herself and she ran towards me, the real me and then BANG.

The next part was played out in slow motion.

The gunman's gun had sparks coming from it. The bullet appeared, and shock waves followed it as it made its way towards Darcey. She turned around in real-time, she could see the bullet coming for her. Her eyes froze in fear. Tears filled the corners of her eyes. She closed them awaiting her fate, tears rolling down her face now in slow motion.

When she finally opened her eyes, the bullet was right in front of her frozen in time.

"It doesn't have to be this way," I said.

She looked at me, scared stiff. Her eyes moved across to me and then back to the bullet. Slowly she took a step back.

She didn't say anything. Black mascara ran either side of her face.

The coffee shop scene faded away back to the blackness of the still room. The bullet was the last thing to go. I grabbed it and gave it to Darcey, She looked at it remorsefully.

The scene changed to that of a funeral. It was inside a church, and at the front was an open casket. The little girl Caroline lay in it. Her mother was on her knees sobbing uncontrollably at the side of the coffin. A picture of the little girl full of life and good health lay beside the sobbing mother. The corpse was distressing for even me to see, the skin whiter than white. You could see they had tried to give her a splash of colour with makeup, but it was obvious, her bald head and cheekbones protruding, she looked frailer than when I saw her in the hospital. She looked like she had suffered.

Darcey burst into tears, "Oh no please, no. I can't bear it."

"There is also the girl I saved from being raped. Do you want to go and see that take place in a world where iLUMiNO doesn't exist? In a world where iLUMiNO isn't allowed to exist because of you?"

"No, no," she said. "Please don't. I'm sorry. I really am. Please no more."

The scene turned back to the room, the chair and table appeared just where she was, all she needed to do was sit down. I sat beside her. Two adults talking openly.

"Why?" I asked.

"You were my big break," she said. "That's why."

Wiping tears away and smudging mascara across the side of her cheek.

"I have worked hard all my life. I have pushed and delivered and done things in my life, and in my career, things that I didn't want to, but I had to in order to work my way up."

"You were my golden ticket. You gave me a twenty-year jump start on my career. It's a fickle business is journalism. But you gave me a taste of the high life and I wanted more."

"By painting me as the bad guy."

"I was threatened by you. Most of the world is. We don't know what you are capable of, what your intentions are."

"I felt compelled to do something, and the career jump you gave me wasn't enough. I wanted more. I wanted more," she cried. "I'm sorry. I really am. I don't know if I can fix this. I wish I'd have taken the bullet. Maybe the world would be better off without me."

"Darcey, those scenarios will never play out. Not in this timeline anyway. They may have done in other timelines. But this one, I was there to change those events in a positive way."

"I still don't know how I can change things. The media is a powerful tool, one word can change the whole perception of events and change public opinion one way or another."

"Don't I know it. Calling me out as a terrorist, live on television! Yeah, I guess you know your stuff. Let me heal you," I said giving her a tissue that appeared on the table.

"Heal me?" she said, wiping her nose.

"If you give me permission to heal you, I think you will be able to move forward."

"What is this place?" The trauma of the scenes playing out was subsiding and Darcey realised she was no longer in the restaurant, "Where are we?"

"We are in the neutral zone," I said. "Here, time stands still on the outside. Whilst in here I am able to construct events, scenarios if you like and watch them play out. I'm still learning my skills and abilities. If I'd have thought, I could have come here before the bomb exploded and looked at different outcomes. But I didn't. I was naïve. I'm still only human".

"So, what now?" she said, rolling the bullet she still had in her hand between her thumb and forefinger.

"Let me heal you," I said.

"Heal me?" she said again, "I haven't got any injuries."

"Let me heal your heart. I am able to take away all negative energy from within. But I won't do it without your permission."

"That's what the girl said on the news. You asked before you changed her. I don't want to be changed," she said. "I like being me".

"Do you? Do you really Darcey?"

She looked down at the table and shook her head slowly.

"Then let me heal you."

She lifted her head, looked into my eyes, and nodded.

"Go ahead. Do your worst," she said.

Placing two fingers on her forehead, my hand glowing, the dark energy that she had within was being released. Anger, betrayal, jealousy, rage, fear, loneliness. A barrage of negativity attached to these emotions was released.

She took a big breath out as if someone had knocked the air out of her lungs. She looked at me and her eyes lit up. She looked alive; her soul looked like it had been awakened.

"What have you done?" she asked.

"I've released the negativity that was stuck to some of your memories and emotions. Don't worry, you will still feel negative emotions in the future, and you will still remember the ones you have had in the past. After all, it was those feelings, that defined you and made you into the person you are today. The only thing that's changed is they are no longer dragging you down. Emotional baggage, sleepless nights, bad decisions, can now be a thing of the past if you embrace it."

"I feel like a new woman," she said. "I can't thank you enough."

"You can," I said. "You can do the right thing and undo the negative work around iLUMiNO. Let us re-write the future. If you make it right, I will give you first dibs on a full-on interview with me."

"You'd do that?"

I nodded, "Promise."

She smiled. I stood and took my seat at the other end of the table.

"Are we going back now?" she asked.

"Ready when you are."

She smiled and gave me a nod.

Suddenly, the black room began to light up one pixel at a time, the waiter appeared, and then the background to the restaurant, and then items on the table, followed by my friends, and then life carried on just as we left it.

Darcey looked over at me as Aaron. She said nothing, as she slowly held the bullet up to me from the neutral zone.

"How?" I didn't have time to finish my question, she dropped the bullet into her handbag then pulled out a wad of notes. Standing up she put them on the table.

"Darlings it's been a wonderful time, and I have very much enjoyed your company, but I have to leave I have things I need to do. I'll take care of the bill, please, it's my way of..." she paused. "Well, it's my way of saying thank you."

Leigh stood up, "Don't, you can't leave yet!"

"Aaron," she said looking at me across the table.

"Its ok guys," I said. "I've done my bit."

Darcey turned around and looked at us all at the table, a realisation hit her across the face. She had realised they all knew my secret. With a nod of understanding, she turned to leave.

"I'll be seeing you. But right now, I have an important interview to schedule with iLUMiNO," Darcey said as she turned and walked out of the building.

"What did you do?" Barkley asked.

I sat there and smiled back at my gang.

"I healed her," I said.

TWENTY SIX
The Interview

I was nervous. I really was. I trusted that Darcey was going to do the right thing. The news was worldwide.

'Darcey Dyson an interview with iLUMiNO.'

Barkley wanted to go with me, but I told him how strange that would look, iLUMiNO, Barkley and Darcey Dyson all in the same place again.

I looked at my birthday cards on the sideboard. I'd put them all up and I admired them. Mum and Dad's card was gone. I'd put it away. Instead, I had the cards up from my friends. Mum and Dad's card was back in the draw where it belonged. I was beginning to heal.

It was 6:55 pm. The interview was scheduled for 7 pm. I poured myself a shot of vodka and drank it neat. Dutch courage. Glancing again at the wall clock in the kitchen, it was now or never. I transformed into iLUMiNO and created a portal directly to the studio. I had learned from my previous portals not to make the oval shape so big. Now you couldn't see where I was coming from in the background. To the observer, it looked like someone was stepping out of thin air. No oval portal, just a line of golden energy and then out pops a leg, arm, and then body.

Arriving at the studio, with five minutes to go before we were supposed to be live on air for the world, I was surprised to see that the studio was in darkness. Normal strip lights high above the studio lights were on, the glitz and glam of the studio were gone revealing it to be what it was, just a normal workspace.

A young guy wrapping cables up with headphones on dropped his cables as he saw me appear out of thin air.

Looking around and helping him pick the cables up, "Where is everyone?" I asked. "I'm...

"iLUMiNO, I know who you are," he said.

"I've got an interview with Darcey in four minutes. Which studio are they in?"

"It's on the rooftop. Did you really..."

That's all I heard as I stepped through the portal appearing just above the rooftop.

I hung there mid-air for about thirty seconds. I could hear a producer or director screaming, "Where is he?" But he wasn't to be seen, this was coming from a walkie talkie.

The set consisted of four lights, with white umbrellas on them, two remote-operated cameras, two armchairs, and a television screen between them in the middle with the news logo on the screen. The only person at the top of the building was Darcey Dyson. She picked up the walkie talkie and replied. "He will be here, trust me".

It was a strange set up for an interview. Yet I felt comfortable with it. I didn't know how it was going to play out, but this was my chance to show the world what iLUMiNO could do for it.

I slowly landed and walked up to Darcey. She shook my hand.

"Hi, you made it. We're about to go live," she said as she clipped on a microphone to my chest. "Are you ready?" she asked as she smiled and pushed her earpiece out of sight from the camera.

I was nervous I will admit, but I nodded and smiled back.

The TV screen between us changed from the news logo to the opening credits. I could hear Darcey as the voice-over, even though the volume was turned off. Another skill of mine, I almost laughed.

The screen was showing clips of me from various sightings. The last one being the footage of me at the Leicester Square bombing. I could hear the producer in Darcey's earpiece, "Live in five, four, three, two..." The screen faded to black and the news logo reappeared.

Darcey looked directly into the camera.

"Ladies and gentleman of the world, iLUMiNO is the name that everyone is talking about. Who is he? What is he? What does he want? Should we be scared? We have taken precautions to make this interview safe." She looked over at me. "You are, after all, a wanted man."

As she said those words, snipers on nearby rooftops around the set made themselves visible and eight armed men wearing bulletproof vests and protective headgear came rushing onto the roof terrace, all raised their weapons and pointed them towards me.

At first, my heart skipped a beat. I was shocked, but not frightened or intimidated in any way. I knew I could leave this place in a fraction of a second, or I could create a hold and stop time by stepping into the neutral zone. I could even instantly go somewhere else if I wanted. I understood why the precautions were in place.

"I understand," I said.

"Right, I know some of these questions have been asked before, but I want this interview to start from the very beginning. Are you human?"

"I am human."

"Would you give some of your DNA to the authorities to prove this?"

"Not willingly, no."

"And why is that?"

"Because I also happen to still lead my normal life. Before what happened to me, the event that made me iLUMiNO, I had a normal life. I still do, and I want to hold onto that aspect of myself."

"Right. Ok, I kind of understand that. So tell me what happened to make you into iLUMiNO?"

"My guide said..."

"You have a guide? Can we see him?"

"I don't think you can see him here physically. Let me try to explain. There are many levels of reality. Scientists have theorised on this, and well, I can only explain it as this... We live in this one, in this reality that is me and you sitting here now having this conversation. What we don't realise is that there are other levels of reality that co-exist within ours."

I paused as I thought and tried to explain it from a different angle. "There are millions of things that exist in our reality but we can not see all of them. Liken it to our electromagnetic spectrum. On the visual aspect, we can see light. However, we can not see gamma rays, X-rays, ultraviolet, infrared, microwaves or radio waves, but we know they exist. I have a guide who exists, but he exists outside of our visual spectrum. But it goes further than that, he exists outside of this reality."

"So this guide, outside of our reality, invisible to us. Is he your mentor?"

"I guess you could say that, yes."

She looks at the camera, as if to roll her eyes, but she gets straight back into the interview. "So let's go back. You said you had, or have a normal life, one without powers and super abilities I assume. So, tell us what happened to you? What was it that made you into the super-powered being you are today?"

"It's called the Schumann Resonance. In scientific terms, it means global electromagnetic resonances which are generated by lightning. The energy is absorbed into the crust of the earth, then discharged from the earth's surface into the ionosphere. I just happened to be in the wrong place at the wrong time. Or maybe it was the right place at the right time, who knows."

"So it was a natural event? You mean to say, this could happen to anyone?"

"The chances of it happening again are nil. It can't ever be recreated again, ever. And one would have to know when and where the next blast of energy would be. Scientists don't have the infrastructure to know when the next blast or beat will be, but they can hear it from outer space. On the space stations, they can tune into the frequency, they call it the earth's pulse."

"What abilities do you have? We know you can fly. We have seen your healing abilities, and you can manipulate objects, not to mention popping in and out of nowhere. Is there anything else you can do?"

"Erm, well right now, I have just learned that I have extra sensitive hearing. The TV monitor there that played the opening credits. I could hear that over your earpiece. What else have I done? Oh, I've walked through solid matter and I can heal myself, as well as others."

"Solid? As in like a wall?"

"Yes, I have walked through a wall. Well, actually, I floated through a ceiling."

I laugh to myself remembering the fall from my rooftop.

"You have been in the limelight for three months now. You are what the world is talking about every day since your arrival. Since the day you saved me from the shooting. Thank you by the way for saving my life." She places her hand on my knee, her gratitude was genuine.

"But the one question on everyone's lips is," she turns directly to the camera and addresses the viewers. "Were you the Leicester Square Bomber?"

As soon as she finished asking the question two more men walked in. The camera zoomed capturing them in the frame. Two police officers, one in plain clothes and the other one in full police uniform. He had these reinforced handcuffs out ready to pounce. The armed men leaned in with their guns aimed directly at me.

I looked at Darcey, and frowned with disappointment. This was my moment, I either disappear, never to return as iLUMiNO or let them take me away. The latter was not going to happen.

"I'll repeat the question iLUMiNO. Did you plant a bomb at the screening of Matrix 4 at Leicester Square cinema?"

"No, I didn't. I have no reason to. I was trying to..."

"Stop, stop right there iLUMiNO! We don't want to hear your explanation!

"But I..." I began to protest.

She leaned forward and placed a finger on my lips.

"You don't have to explain yourself iLUMiNO, because..." She looked directly at the camera. "It was me who planted the bomb."

"Darcey?" I spluttered.

"I wanted to frame you. To turn the public against you. I didn't believe we needed you. I wanted to use you to boost myself further up my career ladder." She leaned in towards the camera, "I am not a bad person. I'm not, honestly."

She pulled out her earpiece, stood up and stepped forward presenting both her wrists out in front.

The plainclothes policeman nodded to his colleague who then placed handcuffs on her. The camera still had its red light on, I knew this meant we were still live. He read out her rights and she was lead off the set.

I sat alone on the outdoor studio news set, the red light was still on the camera, it was still broadcasting live to the world, no one else around just me and billions of people watching. This was my time.

Looking head on into the camera I stood and made eye contact with the world.

"I am here to provide a balance of energies. To rid the earth of negative energy. In doing so, enriching the earth to become a better place to be for all who inhabit it. There is a right and a wrong in the universe, and the distinction is not hard to make. Following the right path, you will find you are much stronger than you think you are. Trust me. I am no saviour or second coming, nor am I your god. I am just like you. A human being with a kind heart. Be the better you".

I smiled directly into the camera, winked at the audience and soared into the night sky. My story had only just begun.

THE ADVENTURE CONTINUES...

I was driving. Mum and Dad would have been so proud. The sun was shining, and the roof was down. I'd bought a Nissan roadster, a two door, two-seater sports car in silver with its sloping fastback style arched roof line and unique brushed aluminium door handles. I felt like a rock star driving it. It was nowhere near as flash as Barkley's new car, but it was mine, and I felt proud as punch driving around.

The UK weather is unpredictable, but the sun was beating down on us and the mixture of the breeze and sun was a perfect combination to stop us from overheating. Barkley sat his sunglasses on top of his head and took a selfie of us. Quickly glancing at the camera, I smiled, then put my eyes straight back onto the road ahead.

Barkley showed me the photo on his phone and we both laughed. "Nice one" he said, then proceeded to post it to his social media.

Without warning, without cause the road ahead of me started to fade out, pixel by pixel and before I knew it Barkley, my car, everything around me had gone within seconds. I was in the neutral zone.

Metatron stood in front of me.

"Aaron, there has been a shift in reality, they are coming for you".

TO BE CONTINUED...

ACKNOWLEDGMENTS

Sarah Jules, Jonathan Cannon: Editors. For whoome if it wanst For Sarah and Jonathan, this book would read very much Like this sentensse.

Glyn Dent: Artist. Created the front cover of iLUMi-NO from my simple words.

Don't miss out!

Visit the website below and you can sign up to receive emails whenever ANTHONY LARKIN publishes a new book. There's no charge and no obligation.

https://books2read.com/r/B-A-BTPN-AAKMB

BOOKS 2 READ

Connecting independent readers to independent writers.

About the Author

Anthony Larkin draws inspiration from such titles as Superman and Perry Moore's Hero.

He graduated from Huddersfield University in 2001 and now balances his writing with his work as a front line registered nurse. In addition, Anthony also writes Pantomimes for his drama academy which is based in his hometown of Barnsley South Yorkshire.

You can find out more about Anthony and the iLUMiNO series by visiting his website

www.ilumino.co.uk

or his Facebook author page www.facebook.com/AnthonyLarkin-Author

Within this book are many hidden references (easter eggs to Superman) how many can you find? Get in touch and let him know.

Read more at www.ilumino.co.uk.

Printed in Great Britain
by Amazon